THE BOUNDARY WATERS

A QUANTUM OPERA

THE BOUNDARY WATERS

A QUANTUM OPERA

GERRY HUERTH

LitPrime Solutions
21250 Hawthorne Blvd
Suite 500, Torrance, CA 90503
www.litprime.com
Phone: 1-800-981-9893

Published by LitPrime Solutions: 06/29/2023

ISBN: 979-8-88703-261-0(sc)
ISBN: 979-8-88703-262-7(e)

Library of Congress Control Number: 2023910125

CONTENTS

CHAPTER 1

He would tell her everything; abracadabra spinning a world around himself, and as long as she could stand it, around her. For a moment, she, Raymona Washington Goldberg, Queen of Doom, opened her eyes to a meager shelter of storied sense that she borrowed from that voice whispering through the phone line. Once again that scepter of a cell phone in hand, she reigned over a world from which she was curiously absent. From a safe 1,500 miles away she listened as he, Matthew Pierson, once again tripped into another story blithely forgetting that once you set a world in motion, it listens patiently for your name, and then sets out to get you.

Sometimes she wondered how so tentative a voice could be so sure of its story. But still his voice droning on about some drama in which he was fool enough to be marooned, was a respite for her, a port of call to which she could visit without having to go ashore. After all she had let go of solid ground years ago and now set her course through wavy solitude, at least as much as anyone living in a rent controlled apartment in New York City can.

Perched in her apartment she kept a wary look out for stories that lurked like reefs just barely below the surface of her life; stories that could tear at her side and then silently, obliviously swallow her up, leaving only the Styrofoam cup on which she had just carved her initials. She could already see that floating obituary bobbing in the sea...all that was left of her self. But still in secret moments she yearned for something solid, the brief sense of destiny that only stories afford...call her sentimental...that's where Matthew Pierson came in.

CHAPTER 2

But then he always had to blow it. He would say, "How are you Raymona?" as if he actually expected her to give him her exact location and lay herself open to who knows what lies waiting in the deep, ready to devour anything that accidentally whispers its name.

That's where popcorn came in; she would fill that expectant silence on the other end of the line with crunchy interference. Burying her hand into that bowl sitting between her thighs, pulling out a large fistful of popcorn; she would stuff her mouth and begin chewing, loose kernels flying in all directions. Between the sound of open mouth crunching and saliva flooding all that debris down her throat, he would get the point. That's one of the things she liked about Matthew, he always got the point...eventually.

On the other end of the line his voice would become vague and slightly penitential, floating away like a helium balloon accidentally released into the sky. Then there would be quiet on his end, like he was watching that balloon of a question become smaller and smaller and finally disappear in the broken hearted blue.

Against all her better judgment, for a brief moment she would relent. From 1,500 miles away she would say, "The usual, I want to place my head on a railroad track and get it over with. No quiet deaths for me; I want to feel it."

A soft quavering sigh of sympathy and maybe awe would filter through from Matthew's end of the phone. "Oh Raymona, that would be terrible. You'd really do that?"

"What's this, a talk show or something? Do I, Raymona Washington Goldberg, sound like one of those pathetic wretches who need to chat about how they're sleeping with their grandmother or their golden retriever in front of six million people, just to get attention? Who do you think I am?"

He was silently walking the short plank of Raymona's patience, breathing very deliberately as if each moment might be his last. Just as she was about to condemn him to the very depths into which she had sent most of her past, she suddenly realized that she would be left all alone onboard. For all her seafaring bravado, she didn't want to be left by herself in the parameters of a life that had been shrinking year by year. Until the blasting, train smashing annihilation which would release her, she needed company or at least stories to mark the time.

For a reckless moment she even wanted to describe the forces impelling her to this gruesome denouement. She itched to once again attempt to find some vindication for her desperate plight, to speak with someone who would nod his head in admiration and sympathy for the undeserved outcome of her life. She grabbed for the popcorn again.

Her body once again froze in its sacrificial posture. Her life must never, never sound interesting; that draws too much attention and lures unexpected danger from the depths. She would rather just silently wait for something that she could anticipate, that far off rumble that at first only she could hear.

Now she waited, head against that cool, iron rail, listening, preparing for that inevitable but coyly reluctant train. Cramped and bored in sacrificial posture, she needed something with which to wile away her time. Her attention began turning from that anticipated doom to Matthew's breathy silence on the other end of the line. Just as he was on the very edge of the plank, she gave him a stay of execution. In her sincerest tone she asked, "How's it hangin', Matthew?"

Now Matthew is a master of the literal. Raymona heard after a very audible sigh of relief, the sound of a chair being pushed out, as if Matthew were standing up to actually looking for something that inadvertently hung from him. He was desperate to answer the question from his sphinx like friend.

Ever the kind soul, she interrupted his frantic search. "Matthew, Matthew, I mean how are you?"

"Me?"

"No, your mother."

"My mother?"

"Let's cut to the chase Matthew."

Matthew gave a short gasp...he got the point. There were a few moments of delicious suspense, as if on his end of the line, he were searching a fabric to find one loose thread with which he could bind Raymona's attention, there...he's got it now.

"You know Raymona, I was at the Uptown Fair last Saturday..."

When he started with "you know", Raymona knew that they were finally in business. His voice whispered out in eerie intensity as if the whole world waited with baited breath to hear this new episode that revolved around him. That voice insinuating familiarity and meaning started winding a spell that included her, but allowed a certain hygienic distance that telephone relationships afford. She stopped eating popcorn and for a while listened, entranced.

"I mean Raymona, do you really want to hear this, it's just something that happened to me?" He drew out the exquisite hunger of Raymona's anticipation.

"Sock it to me Matthew."

She could almost see him. Her need mounted as he carefully fingered that loose thread, frayed and innocently waiting, hidden among all those other threads. There he's got it; he drew it out with such fascination and drama that he once again disappeared into the unraveling.

Raymona quickly but temporarily dropped anchor. Her pleasure always began with his trouble; stories are always trouble.

"Well, I suppose if you really want to hear about this Raymona..."

She didn't even dignify the statement with a response. She had better things to do; the lush melodrama of Matthew's life awaited her. The fact that he was also the master of the long emphatic pause, only heightened her delight. Those long silent intervals were filled with the suggestion that there was so much left unsaid. Raymona soaked up the mystery of the silence. For a few precious moments she could stop worrying about the Danger from the Depths finding her out. The pausing cadence of Matthew's voice drew the Beast far away from her precarious position.

Finally she could relax, nodding in pity and envy, feeling safe for the first time that day. Her life settled into the rhythm of his voice.

"Well, I was with Dick, you know Dick. We were at The Uptown Fair last Saturday; he wanted me to come along. You know it was one of those long summer afternoons that seem to go on forever."

For a moment scales fell from her eyes and she could actually see the sun.

CHAPTER 3

There, there she could pick Matthew out, walking around The Uptown Fair with this friend of somebody he used to work with, you know, Dick.

Uptown, Minneapolis is one of those urban neighborhoods that once had Chinese restaurants specializing in chow mein, sub gum or chicken and dowdy clothing stores, mannequins in the windows gathering dust. A few decades back, store fronts were gutted and turned into an urban mall with an expensive Italian cafe; yogurt shops with a fat free, sugar free flavor of the day; and expensive but casual clothing stores with mannequins too busy changing their attire to gather dust. Green haired kids with rings through various not always appealing parts of their bodies discovered this gentrified paradise and began draping themselves over sidewalks begging for either change or attention. In other words the mall was a success.

To celebrate or perhaps prolong this desperate feat of urban planning, The Uptown Fair filled those streets one weekend every summer. The warm pavement was stuffed with people milling around outdoor booths that sold handmade useless things to hang on walls or from ears. Korean people were selling tacos, and Greek people were selling Cajun food...stories mixed up, swishing and stirring all around; Matthew's kind of place.

Pulled around by Dick, Matthew was floating through that turbulence like some red and white fishing bobber with a secret line and hook hanging underneath baited with his casual innocence. Somewhere between the revolving, pig music boxes and the mirrors set into deer skulls, that red and white bobber began dipping subtly, like something deep down was beginning to draw it in.

"Matthew my man, just the person I was hoping to bump into." A wiry guy all scrunched up in a smile but with eyes still stubbornly sad pulled down Matthew's attention, bobber and all.

Matthew turned towards him with placid surprise. "Arnie, you know I was just thinking about you the other day." Matthew turned ever so confidentially to Dick, who Matthew presumed would be dying to know exactly how this stranger fit into the unfolding drama of Matthew's life. "You know that gay and lesbian contra dance, Dick, well, a few of years ago, I was there on Valentines Day. That's when I met Arnie." Matthew smiled, swept away in the undertow of his newest companion. "Arnie was wearing a black heart pinned to his chest. I just knew I wanted to meet him. A black heart on Valentine's Day, imagine that. We danced and talked, and then I had to leave. You know I had that job at the Hyatt back then; you know the one where I had to clean rooms after people checked out. We've been bumping into each other a couple of times a year since then. Isn't that amazing?"

The vague look on Dick's face made it clear he didn't quite get the point, or perhaps he understood that a story was unfolding in which he did not have a part. Not that in the future Matthew wouldn't periodically bump into him and be amazed by the coincidence.

Matthew was already sailing off, Arnie doing the pulling. Dick melted away into the crowd.

Matthew's smile opened out to the summer afternoon and the antics and stubbornly sad eyes of his new companion. With Matthew's slightly thinning hair dyed (not that he had that much gray to hide) a honey gold color and with a face so placid and receptive it barely seemed to age, he knew that modest silence was the perfect response to the eagerness of his new friend.

"I am pretty unforgettable." Arnie winked as his whole body sprung into a little dance, all for the entertainment of his honey haired guest. Arnie's face was in commotion now; even the patches of mossy, gray brown hair that stuck out of his head like irregularly placed islands, jostled among themselves. "Matthew, I'm going camping next month to the Boundary Waters for five days with a couple other guys, and I wonder whether you'd like to come along?"

This was where Matthew did his Miss America number; surprised and misty eyed at being chosen, humble even, with the kind of humility that only the frequently chosen can manage.

"Arnie what a wonderful idea! It sounds a little scary, five days that's pretty long...well, I think I'd like to go, but I've never canoed before, and I'm not much good at that kind of stuff...do you still want me?" Matthew's eyes gazed out modestly beneath his faux golden hair.

Arnie rose chivalrously to the role of champion. "I'll show you how to do all that. I'd love it if you'd come; you gotta come."

His voice lowered as if he were letting down Matthew softly. "Besides we need a fourth."

Was it the word "love?" Suddenly it was a done deal for Matthew. He missed the whole part about being needed as a fourth; after all this was to be his story. "Well, that sounds pretty wonderful, Arnie."

Arnie sobered and his scrambling features began sinking, perhaps under the weight of a complex explanation. "A few of us go up to The Boundary Waters the first week of August...it's kind of a thing we do each year. One of the guys has AIDS. This is probably his last trip."

Matthew always wanted "a few of us" to include him. He could imagine himself with three hearty guys, carrying canoes, building fires, all the while talking about the depths of his very own psyche. He loved to get familiar. His acceleration into excitement suddenly hit a roadblock. "His last trip, oh..." Matthew's voice tapered off as if the idea of a last trip were unimaginable. Then he applied his sympathy as generously as his honey gold dye. "That sounds so, so hard for him!" Matthew looked solemn, as if his own story were taking on a heightened brilliance, illuminated by the drama of someone else's tragedy.

CHAPTER 4

There was a long pause over the phone line. Despite her vigilance, Raymona too, had a certain yen for the tragic, other peoples' of course. Tragedy made such a distracting story. Of course it had to be filtered through the wavy, impersonal wonders of electronics. Though she kept broadening the physical moat around herself, some vague dissatisfaction stirred within her most secure moments. Then she would turn her television to the news channel, switch her radio to KDQM, the pounding home of rap music, and lie in bed lulled by the fall of western civilization. Even though she took a certain satisfaction in the spectacle of doom on her television set, something still stirred inside her.

A voice, a question poked out of the stillness of her telephone receiver. "Now if I've told you this already, you know, be sure to stop me, Raymona. I wouldn't want to bore you or anything. By the way, how have you been?"

As her hand tightened around her cell phone with menacing intensity, she knew that she wasn't out of the dark yet. Or was this just Matthew's attempt to enhance her pleasure?

Despite Matthew's almost absolute absorption in the spinning and telling of his own stories, he seemed to unconsciously, 1,500 miles away, try to tease her out of her lair. His story paused tantalizing her with suspense. His voice then sprang out at her, unbidden. "Is it as hot in New York as it is here?"

Since it wasn't spring, and nowhere near a holiday, Raymona again foolishly relented. Something inside her momentarily fell into his trap. Against her better judgment, she spoke. "I get sick to my stomach of all this crap."

Like spinning down a maelstrom, she found herself feeling a compulsion to describe her PMS in lurid detail and how she wanted to pour gasoline over her latest therapist, ending the session with a lit match.

As she imagined her therapist bursting into flames, alarm bells rang. Her heart began pounding; ready to explode out of her ears as she realized that once again she had placed herself in terrible jeopardy...she had talked about her life as if it were important. She could already feel the terrible punishment reserved for people who imagine their lives had meaning. The eyes of the Beast were upon her.

Panicking at the folly of her lapse, she fiercely snapped herself out of that false yearning for human communion and shoved popcorn into her mouth.

The sound of hostile crunching exploded into Matthew's ear. Those crunching sounds overwhelmed any fitful sense of curiosity on his part. Duly chastened, he got the point once again and returned to his story.

Popcorn really was the answer. As his tale again began wending its way, the commotion of her jaws began decreasing.

That summer afternoon in Minneapolis pulled them both back. "Could you give me your number, Matthew?" Arnie's body surged with energy, hands flying simultaneously into all his pockets, scattering little hunks of paper around him. "I've got paper and pen somewhere."

Matthew nodded demurely.

Arnie finally discovered a much folded piece of paper with someone else's name and number on the other side. Somewhere in that search he had located a pen which he now clicked with triumph. He carefully tore the paper in half, making sure he kept the piece with the other mysterious name and phone number. Not that he necessarily needed that information now.

Then it was over. The swirling stories all around, drew them both apart. Matthew bobbed on; Arnie scurried off patting the pocket that held two little pieces of paper with two telephone numbers, one of the numbers probably now unnecessary.

The story jolted to a stop. "You know Raymona, there's someone at my door. Imagine that. Well I suppose I better call it quits for now. I sure hope your stomach feels better."

She knew how to pace herself once a story started. Two days later her phone rang. This first human voice that she had heard in two days touched a nostalgic chord. "What do you want?"

"Oh Raymona, how are you?"

"I asked first!"

"Well I was just thinking about you. Were your ears itching?"

"Why in the fuck are you talking about ears?"

"I just wondered if you were all right."

She froze in place. After all the slightest breeze of sympathy would nudge her fragile craft over the edge of the world and into the mouth of the Beast. She could already feel herself spinning down into the depths of terror, voices and sounds blurring into panic, the dominion of her self shattered into an endless meaningless scream.

She needed Matthew's story and now!

The soft cadence of Matthew's voice resumed. Her knees stopped shaking; she could almost relax.

"You know Raymona, guess what happened…it's amazing."

"I hope so Matthew, I really hope so."

"Well, I've really decided to go camping with that bunch of guys! This one guy named Arnie really wants me to come along."

"You're kidding, tell me all about it. I don't want to miss a thing."

He began unraveling his yarn, and she felt securely anchored at her port of call.

CHAPTER 5

Matthew walked home through a warm afternoon that even at 5pm seemed endless. So far north, the summer sun seemed stuck in the blue sky as if the passing moment were an endless kingdom. Only those shadows sneakily but inexorable lengthening and that annoying little twinge in his left knee nudged Matthew with the insistence of time passing. He countered his senses quickly with the anticipation of his latest adventure. He got home just in time to avoid the coming coolness of evening. He didn't notice that the orange day lilies that bordered the front steps had already closed for the day. Their brilliant flags of orange were already twisted into mush.

He stepped into the timeless mustiness of that old duplex in which he lived, and walked upstairs; he decided to glance at his cell phone again to see if he had any messages. After all he could never have too many stories. All those hopes interwove, blurring so that even he could never really tell where an individual story started and stopped. He spun a huge, vague web around himself, that whole interwoven shelter created by so many stories, each story a little eternity bound by hope.

He listened to the very first message. "Hi Matthew, this is Arnie; just wanted to make sure your number worked. Why don't you give me a call? I'll be here all evening and we can start making plans."

Matthew loved to make plans, anything to keep that safe firmament of anticipation over his head. The more intense the drama, the more securely the stars were fixed in that very idiosyncratic night of his. It wasn't so much that he was insensitive or even superficial, he just needed to use whatever energy he could muster to maintain that world he built around himself. Typhoons in Bangladesh, burgeoning romances, AIDS, travel plans; each was little star, a story that somehow added to the luster of his night domain. And as for Raymona she was his librarian or even accountant, someone from that vague world outside his starry web who seemed to be able to chart those tiny points of light.

But sometimes he too felt a niggling yearning for something more, moments when his senses unaccountably opened to a world of sounds and smells...something stirred ever so briefly inside. For a moment the prospect of life somewhere outside his tales and yet somehow within himself, would send him spinning in vertigo. Time to call Raymona. She would understand or at least she needed him. Of course as soon as Raymona caught even a whiff of the sense that Matthew was deluded enough to think that she needed him the conversation would come to a screeching stop.

After all, she had it with needing people, as for their stories...pure foolishness, dangerous foolishness. She only graciously indulged Matthew out of nostalgic pity. She had had it with her own stories; she deserved some sort of reprieve. You see, she came from a long line of storytellers, whole peoples swamped by trouble.

Back in the early sixties, Isaiah and Fay Goldberg were in Alabama; he was a nervous Jewish boy with a yearning for causes that would get him out of the Bronx. Fay Goldberg, formerly Fay Schmidt, was a nice German Catholic girl tired of being good in Yonkers. They met and fell in love on a Freedom Bus Ride just outside of Mobile, Alabama. Between choruses of "We Shall Overcome" and "Cumbuya" something gelled between them. After pledging their commitment to zero population growth they decided to get married and adopted a one year old child named Raymona, from another passenger on that bus, Arnetta Washington, who wanted to try her hand at the freedom offered by The Mobile Academy of Beauty. It was a thoughtless time.

For Isaiah and Fay, the Freedom Bus soon ran out of gas; they moved with the newest addition to their family up to Tarry Town, New York, conveniently tucked way up the Hudson River well beyond the ethnic transformations taking place in the Bronx and Yonkers. Isaiah and Fay continued to be paying members of the American Civil Liberties Union, but now Isaiah jumped on The American Express to become a corporate lawyer; and Fay who always did appreciate the finer things in life, sold real estate in the affluent suburbs north of New York City. For the first two years, Arnetta sent baby clothes to Raymona, and then that stopped. Despite Fay and Isaiah's liberal linings, they weren't really curious about that relationship ending.

Isaiah and Fay had more important things with which to be concerned; Isaiah began sneaking off to synagogue on Friday evenings and Fay began meandering to Mother of Mercy Church on Sunday mornings. Both of them brought Raymona. In addition to this schedule they would alternate bringing Raymona to The Heart of Africa in the Bronx inspired by Malcom X. there she learned dancing, drumming, and slang.

At first the mélange of a life that Raymona called herself seemed amusing and even cute to her parents. At five years of age, she was the hit of the Goldbergs' cocktail party circuit saying things like "Get down mamma," and "Can you dig it?"

By age eight, she became more expressive, perhaps under the influence or confluence of three streams of culture. She became a veritable minstrel of stories. At The Heart of Africa she talked about the vicissitudes of the stock market and the importance of Zionism. At schul she explained that her new Muslim name was Fatima, and that God impregnated Mary leaving her virginity intact. In Sunday school she described the importance of the Roe-versus-Wade Decision and the teachings of The Prophet. Suddenly she was not very popular, spinning recklessly in an out of the gravity fields of her progenitors, picking up debris and disapproval with each rotation. She began to have her first inkling about the danger of stories.

She was awash in them. At age twelve she decided it was time to simplify and began studying chemistry. It seemed so safe to play with those little dead atoms that couldn't complain, even when they were smashed. At least they didn't have a story to tell; they simply followed rules. She was finally safe behind glass watching those arid firmament of physical laws move the grand clock we call the universe. The chain of cause and effect had already been set inexorably in motion leaving no room for whining stories.

And when computers came along she was in heaven. It's either yes or no, you either follow the program or you don't. There's no in between place with computers. And as she already knew, the in-between-places, the boundaries are where stories spread like the plague. She knew that people's puny thoughts had no bearing on that beautiful machine. How splendid, how simple, no human mess, none at all.

If it was such a happy ending, you might ask why does she now spends most of her time in a tiny rent controlled apartment watching television, clicking her ball point pen to rap music, eating popcorn, and listening to the voice of that Typhoid Mary of stories, Matthew Pierson.

It's not a pretty tale...she was minding her own business studying for her first final at Columbia

University, to which she had gotten a full scholarship. In fact she had become a media star at her alma mater. If you look at any of the recruiting brochures from that liberal era, you'll see her brown face popping up everywhere like a mushroom. There she is in the chemistry department surrounded by those mostly pale, male faces that look like they need a haircut or at least a fashion consultant.

In fact the frenzy to include her was sweeping the whole campus. There she was, innocently studying the details of this huge mechanism of the universe, and all the time the National Organization of Women, the Black Panthers, B'nai B'rith, and even the Catholic Newman Club all claimed her as their own.

She redoubled her concentration on the Periodic Table of Elements, but unknown to her, even the foundations of this last bastion was silently eroding. Even today she sometimes wonders what would have happened if she had only minded her business counting molecules and finding new ways to get the ink spots out of blouses. But no, perhaps all the varied accolades from campus were impairing her judgment; she decided to become a renaissance woman and took a minor in physics. If only she knew then, what she knows now, she might be contentedly working in a laboratory somewhere discovering a new sugar substitute.

She began plowing through physics books. You can imagine her shock and disbelief when there, right in front of her eyes in bold naked print she saw something called THE UNCERTAINTY PRINCIPLE. At first she thought it was a joke snuck into that textbook by some bored writer who was trying his hand at comedy. Then frantically she looked in the index of the other physics textbooks and there it was again... THE UNCERTAINTY PRINCIPLE.

She broke out into a cold sweat, her body shivered while the outside world began shimmering; but she forged ahead. If she were meeting her doom, she wanted to face it head on; she kept reading. It turns out that one of her mothers people, a fellow German, thank you Fay, named Werner Heisenberg had discovered that on the sub atomic level our view of things becomes whacko, not because of the imprecision of our tools of exploration, but because of the nature of that Alice in Wonderland world: the more you focus on one thing, the more the other things become blurry, never can you get a complete picture; nature sits there vaguely smiling like one big fat Cheshire ambiguity.

Raymona was aghast to find that studying physics was like holding on to a balloon full of water; certainty was always squeezing out of grip and swelling beyond grasp. If you measure the speed of a subatomic particle you cannot find its location. If you measure the location of a subatomic particle you can't measure its speed... swell! The looser grip of probability is the only way of getting a general picture. You kind of loosen your certainty of individual parts, blur your eyes and get a probable picture of the whole...probable! Circling clouds of probability, instead of discrete intricate mechanical orbits...what is the world coming to?

But things got worse; in that weird world; in here and out there start to get all mixed up too. A whole menagerie of ideas began springing up in that bizarre boundary called Quantum Mechanics. If only she had never heard that name. Two electrons at different end of the universe could communicate with each other instantaneously as if distance didn't matter. They become entangled by some mysteries mode of connection beyond time and space. She even learned that measuring is suspect, the intent of the viewer affects the outcome of the experiment. What a mess! Measuring, that most innocent, benign, sweet occupation that had allowed her to separate herself from the world was shimmering away.

What happened to that beautiful machine, that predictability humming away? Isaac Newton where are you? The grid on which her salvation had rested was already going the way of dodos, hula-hoops and the single income family.

Then she learned that Europe, that spawning bed of countless stories...wars, revolutions, and clothing styles, had done it again. In Switzerland, one of her father's people, thank you Isaiah, Albert Einstein, had actually started mixing up space and time turning Newton's machine into silly putty. Now there was this preposterous and unimaginable thing called space-time. Time, that impervious and absolute measure, waxes and wanes depending on your speed. Energy and matter could be converted into each other in some sort of coy dance of transformation.

Africa too was seeping in everywhere; geneticists

were suggesting that all of us were grandchildren of some woman in Africa who lived 200,000 years ago. There was even talk of creating a special holiday named after Martin Luther King. . .another holiday was the last thing that anyone needed. White boys started swiveling their hips, and music started to escape its measures, voices and instruments pulling us into a way of life that danced instead of marched. She hated dancing!

Stories, stories everywhere started to rush through the dikes of her world. She said goodbye to pen holders, slide rules, and molecules; switching her major to journalism. This was a desperate maneuver, but she knew now that there was no place that was safe from the plague of stories. She decided that maybe, just maybe, she could use her word processor to hold all those stories at arms length. Perhaps she could shelter herself behind the impermeable membrane of the press and keep other peoples' troubles at arms length by writing about them.

When everyone else in her Journalism 101 class searched for significant stories about politics, sex, or national security, she explored smaller stories like the inverse relationship between national reading scores and the proliferation of designer jeans. She wrote a scathing article about the humanitarian betrayal that Fruit of the Loom was perpetrating...it was starting to advertise and sell colored men's underwear. In fact men all around the country were beginning to notice their underwear. Not that she had any intimate contact with men or anybody for that matter, but she saw commercials and even store mannequins trading those discrete graying stained banners for flashier fare, garish accouterments called designer underwear. Walking down the street Raymona could pick out those men who had succumbed. They would have smug little smiles on their faces as if they were the sole possessor of a dramatic secret. Even worse, women encouraged them. Her sisters throughout the western world who had long ago been forced to submit to fancy lingerie by a patriarchal culture interested in turning women into seductive stories, now actually encouraged the spread of this disease to men. Gallantly she blew her journalistic whistle as institution after institution succumbed to stories. All to no avail.

Clutching her diploma, major in journalism, minor in chemistry, she set out to defiantly meet the insolence of change in New York City. Forgetting about hubris, she thought that she was strong enough behind her journalistic barricade to face that naked city with nine million stories. She got a job at a small publishing company as a copy writer. And that's where fate smiled on her ever so briefly. There she met Matthew Pierson, at her very first quixotic foray into the world of adulthood.

At this company that barely limped through the competitive world of publishing (in fact it was eventually sold to a dry cleaning empire), Raymona was making her way. She was stuck at the dizzy height of the 25th floor with all her whining coworkers; she knew that something terrible was bound to happen to one of those story addicted victims. With heart pounding panic, she realized that she wasn't just writing about stories but was actually marooned on the 25th STORY. She spent a lot of time around the water cooler; it was next to the exit sign.

There she was on that fateful day, wild eyed, figuring out what to do if a plane crashed into the building or King Kong went on the rampage again. That's when this short, well scrubbed, light haired guy who looked like he was too young to drive, let alone earn a living, came up to that water cooler. She began sticking her elbows out, bristling to protect her position by the stairway.

Blind to the danger of those lethal elbows, he looked at her with familiar intimacy, as if she were his lifelong companion and they had just woken up together from a rather comfortable snooze. "You know, if I drank as much water as you, I'd be in the bathroom all day. I have a very weak bladder."

For a moment even Raymona was dazed. Then she looked back at him and saw obvious admiration for her bladder capacity in those large, trusting eyes. Practically wagging his tail, he stuck out his hand. "My name's Matthew. I work in the Arts and Leisure Department, I'm glad to meet you."

Finally not wanting to make a scene, she grabbed his hand and shook it, telling him that her name was Raymona and that she was new around here.

He looked at her like they were the last two people on earth and said, "I sure hope you like it around here Raymona."

And for a moment she hoped that she actually would like it there too.

Then he smiled like he was reassured, and she had something to do with it. "Well I guess I better get back to my desk, I'm writing copy for this book called BODY PIERCING AS AN OPPORTUNITY FOR TRANSCENDENCE. What are you working on Raymona?"

For a moment she almost crushed the paper cup in her hand and then thought what the hell, she's talking with someone who describes his bladder size to strangers. "I'm writing a book jacket for something called ARTIFICIAL INSEMINATION, THE FARMER'S FRIEND."

With excitement pulsing in his face, he said, "That sounds really interesting Raymona. I sure hope that you and I can get to know each other real well."

She was cushioned and caught by those trusting eyes. She only realized years later that, that wide eyed trusting look may also have something to do with nearsightedness and his refusal to wear glasses. He thought glasses made him look old. For the next five years they saw each other every work day.

He even began calling her at home, sure that she'd be interested in his latest forays into romance. For her part she began sharing her theories about the insidious danger of stories. He would listen enveloped in hushed silence on the other end of the phone as her theory evolved. She described in lurid detail how stories are larger then any of us, waiting patiently everywhere for an opportunity to pounce on unsuspecting victims. They can hide in the most innocent circumstance or hang on the smallest of objects. Raymona wouldn't even talk to someone wearing a wedding ring. When hapless humans come anywhere near a story, the story, like some expanding amoeba, engulfs and annihilates them. Before they know it, all they can see are the insides of the story's stomach while they're slowly being eaten away and absorbed. Finally they become the story; every ounce of self gone. The story in turn increases in menacing potency.

And those beasts are waiting to pounce everywhere, from taxi's, ear rings, junk mail, from that stranger asking you for the time of day, from those smells coming out of restaurants, from boom boxes, everywhere, everywhere! Thinking she could protect Matthew from the folly of his indiscrete familiarity, she spent hours on the phone with him, like a Cassandra warning of doom.

After listening to her warning forecasts, Matthew would become silent for a moment and then would say, "Wow Raymona, you're so deep. I'm glad you're my friend; you make life seem so interesting."

At the end of five years of working with Raymona in the office on the 25th story, Matthew fell in love with a man returning to Minnesota. AIDS had already pounced upon the gay population in New York and was beginning to devour it. With his lack of resistance to stories, Raymona thought that Matthew abandoned New York for the fresher air of Minneapolis, none to soon. She never could remember all his boyfriend's names anyway. Somewhere along the line what's-his-name disappeared and one year later Matthew was living in his current apartment with a new career...rubbing bodies with oil and ushering people into the New Age. As a sideline he also cleaned hotel rooms.

Matthew was like one of those caged canaries that miners used to bring down into the depths with them to test the air. In spite of his endlessly distracting adventures, he was very sensitive. Now when he woke up at four in the morning with the pestering bladder of a man turned forty, he felt that somehow like the ozone, his protective layer of dramas was wearing thin. In the daytime he managed to forget those nightly rendezvous with middle age, and would be startled, even slightly offended by cashiers addressing him as "Sir." The story of aging was eying him from the depths.

On Raymona's end of the phone line (people still had phone lines back then), the dry cleaning conglomerate that owned her company began suspiciously eying profit margins. A story called "restructuring" started to pounce on employees; then they would simply disappear. Rather than find herself in the beast's belly she decided to do free lance editorial work in her apartment. Goodbye Restructuring. Goodby King Kong. Her life began orbiting closer and closer around the protective mass of her apartment. She continued her editorial work at home. Few links were left to the outside world: her television, her rap radio channel, her telephone, and finally her answering machine with which she screened out the entire world except Matthew. Though by now she had given up any notion of affectively warning Matthew about the danger of his naiveté, she began relishing her new role as the imperial audience in the coliseum of Matthew's far fetched tales. She watched his bloody skirmishes below with the whimsy of a Roman emperor, wondering when she would finish off each story with a casual thumbs' down.

CHAPTER 6

Suddenly that whispering voice from Minneapolis resumed.

Heart pumping frantically she pulled herself out of the morass of storytelling.

Breathlessly he told her that the three voyagers were actually coming to his apartment to talk things over before they ventured into the heart of darkness. "Raymona, I'm so glad that they would come to my house, you know how much I like people to come here. Sometimes, especially lately this apartment seems kind of empty. Even calling you doesn't always help. I get this itching feeling that there needs to be something more going on in here, not that there's lots of people who don't want to see me, but still...you wouldn't want to come and see me again, would you?" There was another dangerous pause.

Just when she thought it was safe, the rug was pulled out from underneath, she started to stumble into danger. Raymona had long since given up on invitations. In fact, Matthew's apartment marked the place of her last sustained visit to the world outside. It was after that fateful visit that she finally decided that probability just wasn't good enough anymore.

She remembered how she had foolishly taken his bait. "You know Raymona, I was just thinking. Why don't you come and see me? We'll have a good time...I'll cook and we'll talk, and you won't need to do anything you don't want to do."

That was back when she still thought she owed the world the wonder of her presence. She boarded the plane to Minneapolis.

He met her at the airport with a handful of daisies... not a good start; flowers are dangerous. How many stories have begun with the reckless gift of flowers? When she walked into the living room of his apartment in that decaying, old duplex, she knew beyond doubt that she was in for trouble. The living room floor of that second story apartment slanted precariously. She knew that any minute she was going to slip down crashing onto the grass outside. The crashing part wasn't so bad, but she didn't want to meet her fate accidentally. She wanted it to be her fault, not some stupid landlord's. To make matters worse, the furniture and the big old rolled up rug were all pushed to the wall of that sinking side. Matthew had been dating this guy who thought the room would look much better with stripped hardwood floors. Somewhere between rolling up the carpet and actually stripping the floors, the guy disappeared.

The living room was just the start of the bad news. He ushered her deeper into his apartment. He had one of those old kitchens with flowered linoleum worn black in spots and a single sink slightly tilted backwards so water never completely drained out. Sort of like his life. He was always trying out exotic recipes because some one gave him a book on Japanese or Ukrainian cooking.

It was bad enough that she had sat for hours with a hundred other accident prone passengers, but now every meal was a dizzy trip to some corner of the world. Because the sink didn't drain completely, the dishes never really got clean. Stale smells from around the globe were always brewing in that kitchen sink, eventually coating the plates and silverware with a greasy international flavor.

Finally she had to tell Matthew that she was on this special diet. She could only eat things that were micro waved in their own packages. She was also allergic to silverware, only new plastic could touch her mouth.

"What an amazing diet Raymona! Do you think maybe I should try it?"

He also had this small room painted dusty rose. During the day there was a procession of men and women to his door downstairs. Matthew would rush down, swing the door open and say breathlessly, "You know I'm so glad you've come." Then he would usher them into the dimly lit rose room, and above the murmurs of new age music he'd whisper, "You can take your clothes off here; I'll be back real soon."

Matthew did massage, although when Raymona called it that, he'd mysteriously but definitively say, "No

Raymona, I do body work. When I lay my hands on a person, something wonderful happens. It's so amazing."

She tried to let him down gently. "Now Matthew, you could get away with that amazing stuff when you wore bell bottom pants and flowers in your hair, but when your gums started receding and your ass deflated, well you've started slipping into the realm of the peculiar." She decided to leave it at that, a word to the not so wise.

She slept in the slanting living room on the sofa pushed against the wall dipping dangerously downward. Matthew slept in an unpainted bedroom that had a view of the alley. Heaps of brown paper bags holding every letter that he had ever received from anybody littered the floor. "You know Raymona you never know when you need things like that. It would be like letting those people down to just stuff their letters in the garbage." So the piles kept multiplying; postcards, love letters, overdrafts, all stuffed in those brown paper bags that eventually became brittle and spilled out their contents.

Rusty lawn furniture cluttered his screened in porch that overlooked the front sidewalk. Raymona didn't go out there, she wasn't much for air circulation, you can never tell what stories might blow in.

On the afternoon of the last day of what she resolved would be the last trip of her life, while staring at his collection of salt and pepper shakers that Julianne left him, you know that aunt that died on the mattress that he slept on; Raymona smelled some new odor coming through the open kitchen window from a big straggly bush. "Hey Matthew what's that big bush outside that stinks?"

"You know Raymona, you may know a lot about the human soul, but you sure don't know much about flowers. That's a lilac bush out their trying its best to let us know it's May. It's amazing isn't it?"

That was enough for Raymona. Give her the exhaust fumes of New York City any day. When she left the next morning, she knew that 1,500 miles was just about the right distance from Matthew and his stories.

When she returned to the safety of her apartment, the two once again settled into their regular and hygienic phone conversations. She could spend hours imagining Matthew's life and what he should do if he had any sense.

His voice whispered on; her grip on the cell phone relaxed.

The voyagers were rendezvousing at Matthew's apartment. Anticipation sparkling in the confines of his imagination, he sat waiting on that porch enthroned on a rusty chair, watching the sidewalk below so intently that even absolute strangers passing by felt compelled to stop in front of his house for a few moments.

Arnie approached first; the mossy, crumbly patches of hair on his weathered head were slicked down. As he walked on the sidewalk below, his whole torso bounced from side to side like a metronome, his sailor legs continually stopping the tilt and pushing him back to the other side.

Matthew rushed down the stairs. "Arnie I'm so glad you've come."

"Hi, Matthew my man."

"Come on in Arnie. How are you? Do you want some tea or mineral water or..." Matthew lost track of the options in the excitement of the welcome.

For a moment Arnie looked down, fumbled, and lifted a paper bag up to Matthew.

Matthew looked strangely excited at the crumbled bag.

"Matty, I brought a six pack for you."

Maybe it's all of Matthew's "you knows," but eventually almost everyone began calling Matthew by different variations of his name, except. Raymona.

"What a good idea Arnie. Why don't you take one, and you know, I think I'll just have one too."

Finally beers in hands, seated on rusty lawn furniture they both peered out as the last afternoon light filtered through the porch screens.

"You know Arnie, I realized last night that I don't know much about you."

Hands fidgeting over his damp can, Arnie looked up at Matthew. One of his droopy eyes winked. "To know me is to love me, Matty my man." He freed one hand up to scratch his hair that was already beginning to spring up in fuzzy patches.

"I like your sense of humor Arnie. When I saw that black heart you were wearing and all...not that, that's not really an important piece of information, but

I don't know what you do or if you live with somebody. I guess I know you like camping, but that's about it."

Arnie's head and neck circled a little before he propped up a smile on his face. "I'm a nurse; I mean a registered nurse." His fingers were drumming nervously on his almost empty can. "And I live with this guy named Lance who I never get a chance to see too much of. I don't know how he has the will power to stay away from me."

No need for Arnie to worry. Matthew was impressed. "That sounds exciting Arnie, your job I mean." Matthew nodded very kindly.

There was a quiet regular knocking on the door downstairs.

Matthew again rushed down in a breathless whirlwind. He swung the door open revealing a tall, precisely thin man with a briefcase stood at the door like some important ambassador. Just as Matthew was collecting enough air to say, "You know, I'm so glad you've come," the stranger lifted his right hand; it hung there for a moment before Matthew realized that he should shake rather than kiss it.

The personage spoke, "My name is James J. Arndt. The "J" is for 'Julius,' but my friends just call me James Arndt. I come from a very old family in Iowa."

"Well thanks for letting me know, James Arndt. My name is Matthew; my friends call me anything they want. You know I'm really glad you came."

As Matthew's voice trailed off, James Arndt passed him, intent on examining the surroundings.

"Arnie's here already, can I get you something to drink, James Arndt?"

"No thank you. By the way, if you put a little linseed oil on the woodwork it would not look so dull and dried out. You can never give woodwork too much care."

James Arndt who had already taken in the layout of the apartment led the way into the porch.

Matthew lagged behind noticing the woodwork for the first time in his life. He rubbed his finger along a groove as if he were plowing some dusty field. "It sure is good to know that stuff about the woodwork, James Arndt."

The light outside was turning a dusty orange and crickets from all over the neighborhood were starting to call to each other.

By the time Matthew stepped onto the porch, Mike and James Arndt were already catching up, their voices calling back and forth to each other.

"How is Lance?"

"He's up to his old tricks."

"Theodore and I missed bowling last week. There was a wine tasting party I could not miss."

"Gutter balls, gutter balls, that's all I had last week, fortunately Lance loves me for my looks. Hey, I ran into Mark the other day. Turns out he and Jack are on the outs."

"According to Ronald, it is much more complicated than that. I am disappointed in Mark. He should know better."

"Ronald?"

"Steve's friend."

"How's Steve?"

"Steve said he's being pursued by this younger person named Lawrence."

"Not Lawrence the hairdresser."

"One and the same."

"I thought Lawrence was with Ron."

Matthew's head turned from one guest to another, smiling at what he hoped were crucial points in their mysterious dialogue. Matthew was at home with blurry mystery.

Just as their words were dissolving into the cricket sounds, Matthew looked from his screened height to the sidewalk below, now a molten orange pathway dappled with evening shadow. A tall figure, slightly limping, walked through the golden passage way. Solemn determination propelled that figure through the twilight. A dog followed cautiously guarding him.

CHAPTER 7

Matthew pulled Raymona back into the present. "It was so amazing! That man approaching looked familiar. Then it all came back to me. I remembered that I had seen him at a gay and lesbian contra dance a few years ago too; I guess the same one I met Arnie at." Matthew was back in his element.

The church hall was bright and warm even though outside the wind was driving sleet down like nails; like spring would never come, but inside the hall that old fashioned, sweet fiddle music was playing and all sorts of men and women were lilting around in circles. That's when that guy entered, tall and rangy, but when he walked into the room that night he carried with him this kind of feeling of being curious and daring, like a boy who grew into a man without having to pretend too much, like someone who didn't need to be asked out on an adventure, because he had plans of his own. He looked straight out ahead, his body loping, but alert and ready to spring, kind of handsome too, straight hair hanging almost to his shoulders, not like a pop star, all self conscious, but like Davy Crocket, hair kind of hacked off, king of the wild frontier, you know.

Guys just kept circling around him casual like, trying to get his attention. He was so unselfconscious, like he didn't even know that everyone was revolving around him. He didn't seem smug or anything, but he took all that attention in stride like it was his birthright. Matthew didn't even consider asking him for a dance, he was just way beyond Matthew. That's when someone else asked Matthew to dance, Arnie. But once and a while that evening, Davy Crocket would lope by in all his grace, and for a second Matthew's heart flew open. Arnie said his name was Daniel, or as Arnie called him, Dan the Man.

"Well Raymona, so who should this guy walking out of the evening be?"

At this point Raymona would know that Matthew was building up to some not so amazing revelation. Kind soul that she was, she would allow silence on her end of the phone line to intimate a feeling of suspense.

"Cut to the chase, Matthew." Raymona finally spoke.

"Daniel, you know, Dan the Man, that guy from the contra dance."

The story was really revving up. Now he stood at the screen window watching the figure come nearer. Despite the long strides, there was a kind of snag that seemed to catch the approaching figure mid step that only stubborn determination could push through. His face...the horizontal sun shone against the planes of a face drawn tightly like dry hide on a drum. There was something secret about him like he didn't want anyone to know the price he was paying for those long strides. Only his dog could notice.

Matthew turned away from the forbidden sight just as Arnie said, "Here comes Dan."

Before rushing down those stairs, Matthew took a secret moment to examine Arnie and James Arndt; they seemed pretty healthy. Dan, Dan must be the guy with AIDS. This is his last camping trip.

This time Matthew descended down those stairs more slowly, trance like. The cross currents of the anticipated meeting spun Matthew into an eddy of reflection.

Just before Matthew swung the door open, he tried to recall what it was like to meet an ordinary person. The door opened, the last sun of the day streaming horizontally silhouetting a tall opaque figure.

"I'm glad you've come. I'm Matthew." He rested his eyes on that shadowy face long enough to begin making out features, then put his hand out. As they touched, Dan looked away to recover his breath and push aside that desperate look from his eyes. By the time Matthew said, "Come on in Dan...Arnie and James Arndt are already here," Dan had shorn up his composure.

Dan nodded. His brown fringe of hair stirred as he loped into the duplex. "This is Trixie. Do you have a bowl or something for water? This warm weather really does her in. Doesn't it Trixie?"

She wagged her tail at the sound of her name,

glancing up as if to reassure him that the privacy of his fatigue was maintained. "Sure Dan. I'll get some right away." Dan followed Matthew up the stairs.

He motioned to Dan. "Why don't you two go into the porch?"

Matthew walked into the kitchen. Trixie guarded Dan's way.

By the time Matthew returned with the water, the party in the porch was in high gear. Arnie was rolling his eyes, while clutching his empty beer can slowly crushing it. "Dan, you old queen, you made it! You can't get out of this trip. We need somebody to carry all the supplies."

For a second Dan caught Arnie's eyes and looked grateful and then covered it up with laughter. "I can't help it you're such a pussy and need a real man on your trip."

Trixie, who had strategically placed her back to Dan, positioning herself between him and the others, relaxed at the sound of his laughter and started glancing at the bowl of water...all clear.

James Arndt looked up as if to bestow approval on the company.

Arnie held the floor, eyes, face, hands, feet, each caught in different dance steps. The commotion of a clown filled the room. "Do you remember last year when John came along?"

James Arndt perked up and began sedately laughing, a tasteful joke clearly understood.

Matthew nodded, trying to smile.

Arnie knew he had his audience. "He wanted to bring tomatoes into the Boundary Waters. Can you imagine it? First time he slipped every single one of those tomatoes smashed and seeped into the bag with his underwear."

Dan was catching the momentum. "He looked like he had a bad case of hemorrhoids."

James Arndt nodded complacently. "I kept telling him he had the wrong skin coloring to wear red."

Arnie captured those loose conversational ends and turned to Matthew. "Each year we invite some new victim to go camping with us."

All eyes turned on Matthew.

There he was, carefully ensconced in thoughts about this amazing trip with three guys, one of whom was Dan the Man, and now they were all looking at him, prodding him with their laughter, like they knew something that he didn't.

He smiled at those faces staring at him, hoping they would appreciate his apologetic embarrassment.

Matthew took his cue from Trixie who was congenially lying next to Dan's chair, eyes half open, but ears propped up at right angles taking in all the sounds of the evening. Matthew relaxed the grin on his face and settled back into the anonymity of a knowing placidity, all the time listening alertly to prevent himself from creating another uncomfortable scene.

Still ironic, but softening into kindness, Dan's voice interrupted the humor. "Matty have you ever been camping in the Boundary Waters before?"

Matthew was very careful not to stare at Dan too long, lest that story about Dan slip out before it was mature. He carefully measured out looks to both Arnie and James Arndt. "You know, I never really have."

Arnie took over. "We'll show you the ropes. Won't we guys?" His feet were scampering on the floor. "Do you guys remember Steve, two years ago? He kept wondering where the showers were."

James Arndt sat up very straight. "There are rules in the Boundary Waters, Matthew."

Matthew found himself straightening too and nodded ferociously.

In measured tones James Arndt continued. "The Boundary Waters are pristine wilderness…we have to be very careful. You cannot carry glass or tin cans into the area. Any trash you generate, you need to bring out with you. There are no showers or faucets. All the water that you drink comes from the lakes. You cannot drink lake water unless it is chemically purified or boiled. The water up there is contaminated by a micro organism called giardia. Giardia swim around in the Boundary Waters just waiting to get into the intestinal track of careless campers. Giardia take up residence there, swimming around and hooking on to the intestinal walls. The intestines become irritated and spasm, propelling their entire contents out in a continuous and vulgar way."

Matthew's eyes were now wide open, straining to see those vicious little giardia swimming from somewhere beyond the horizon of his hopes. He didn't want to feel alien creatures in his intestines hooking into his life. The fact that something was lurking out their just waiting to involve him in a story in which he would spend most of the time on the toilet, seemed utterly horrible.

"Now Matthew," James Arndt was on a roll, "some years back some thoughtless vacationer brought a dog along who was infected with giardia. For a moment he stared at Trixie, as if she bore responsibility for her species.

She must have noticed his glare; she gave a little jerk and ferociously began snuffling her groin.

Dan took Trixie's cue and changed the subject. "Do you have a sleeping bag?"

Matthew slipped into innocent looking bewilderment. If he could have cocked his ears like Trixie he would have, anything to catch Dan's canine loving attention. "You know Dan, I never went camping before, I'm not sure where I can get a sleeping bag." Dan's face relaxed into a smile, as if he wanted to pat Matthew's head to reassure him. "Matty, I'll drop off a pack this week."

Arnie's body parts began jangling. "Let's get down to business and show this tenderfoot how it's done."

James Arndt placed his briefcase on his lap and with a precise click opened it withdrawing three crisp pieces of paper. He handed them out carefully like ballots. "Now I want you to examine the paper carefully. As you look from left to right, you will see two vertical lists. Each list has a heading. The first heading from the left is 'SUPPLIES FOR WHICH EACH CAMPER IS RESPONSIBLE.' The second heading towards the right reads 'GENERAL SUPPLIES.' I'll read off the 'GENERAL SUPPLY' list first. Again this is the list towards the right." He took one critical look at Matthew to ascertain if his attention was properly moored. Then James Arndt began a litany to which Dan and Arnie kept answering "Got it."

Matthew felt like he should chime in too, but come to think of it, he really didn't have things like lanterns, camp stoves, tents, let alone canoes.

"Now I'll begin with the second list, the first list on the left entitled 'SUPPLIES FOR WHICH EACH CAMPER IS RESPONSIBLE.'" James Arndt drew out the world "RESPONSIBLE" and fastened it on Matthew.

Matthew wanted to pass this test.

"Rain gear."

This was Matthew's chance. "I have this jacket that works pretty well when it drizzles."

Arnie intervened. "I have an extra."

"Toiletries."

"Oh ya, I sure have those." Matthew told himself that this wasn't so bad after all.

"Insect repellant and sun screen."

Matthew looked uncertain for a moment.

James Arndt smiled benevolently. "Of course you know Matthew that you can get that at any drug store, but if you really want the very best products go to Midwest Mountaineering."

Matthew nodded appreciatively.

"One water proof canvas sack."

"I've got this canvas bag I got free from the airlines a few years ago. I've been storing letters in it."

The three began laughing.

Arnie paused in mid stream and looked at Matthew. "I have an extra, I'll drop it off."

"Food for one supper."

Matthew expanded hopefully. "I really like experimenting with recipes."

Arnie again resumed his place in center stage. "You don't have to be Betty Crocker, Matty. I'll call you this week and explain things. It's really a piece of cake."

James Arndt caught the culinary pun and nodded to Arnie.

The list droned on, but Matthew pushed all his questions to that future call from Arnie. And then it was over...that wasn't so bad.

Finally after James Arndt carefully crossed off the last word from the last list, Arnie took charge again. "Okay gang, we'll meet at my place, Sunday at 8a.m. Be there or be square."

With unbidden gallantry, Dan said, "I'll pick up Matthew."

Matthew was thrilled, but nodded placidly at Dan.

Just as the three were beginning to resume their lore from years gone by, Matthew noticed Dan starting to gradually deflate in his chair. First his smile drained away, then his body began sinking as if his bones were softening, and finally his eyes began emptying.

Trixie sat up and stationed herself closer to him.

Arnie glanced over at Dan secretly. "Well, I have an early morning tomorrow. I guess we'll have to call it quits. I'll have to deprive you guys of my company. Can't stay here all night."

Dan perked up a little bit. "Well, I guess I'll call it a night too."

Then as if he heard a school bell, James Arndt began carefully collecting his papers; he placed the tidy pile in his briefcase and clicked it closed.

Under the camouflage of that distraction, Dan propped himself up into standing position. Trixie wouldn't take her eyes off him.

James Arndt stood up, flicking imaginary crumbs from his lap. "I saw John McGee last week."

Arnie stood up, an imaginary bowling ball in his hand, walked a few steps and released the ball with a swing. "How's John's score with Ray? Strike I hope?"

Since Matthew felt that he had somehow passed the test of the two lists, he decided to ask about one of the mysterious names. "Who's John McGee?"

James Arndt cocked his head in appraisal. "Don't you know? He is Terry's friend."

"I suppose so." Matthew didn't know who Terry was, but didn't spend too much time wondering because out of the corner of his eye he was following Dan out the door. Not that he released his more direct gaze from James Arndt who by this time was examining the woodwork again as he made his exit.

Arnie lingered out in the porch pacing as if he were

actually setting out on that early morning of his, but still circled, tethered to some sort of expectation of the evening.

Matthew noticed him when he went out to the porch to pick up the bowl that Trixie used. "Oh Arnie, what a nice bunch of guys. I think it's going to be all right."

"Would I ever mislead you Matty?" Arnie continued following his well worn circular groove.

"Oh by the way Arnie, does Dan have a partner?"

Arnie's face went slack. "Ya, he does...Francis." He stopped pacing. "I guess I better be leaving. I don't want to overwhelm you with my charisma."

CHAPTER 8

Raymona knew that the story-beast had Matthew's name, in fact it was circling closer and closer. She could tell, because the intervals between his calls began to decrease.

"You know Raymona, that camping trip I told you about?"

"Do you mean the outing with Jack The Ripper and his buddies?"

"Jack who?"

"Anybody who wears black hearts on Valentines Day and drags dying people out on camping trips may be just a little bit on the, shall we say, the ghoulish side. How many times do I have to remind you to stay in the house on Valentine's Day?" Of course she knew Matthew wouldn't follow her advice...thank god!

"Now be serious Raymona. This is important."

She could tell by the drama percolating up through his voice, that the game had started in earnest. She pushed her popcorn bowl aside, satisfied that in spite of his impending doom, he would be distracting the beast long enough for her to have a few moments of safety. Matthew made such a commotion that any story lurking around would be lured to his doorstep. Matthew Pierson died for our sins.

"This is really important Raymona. There's this guy named Dan who's coming along. He's the guy with AIDS. I feel so funny about him. I feel all full and empty at the same time. You know how it is on an early October afternoon when leaves are yellow like they're trying to hold on to the summer just a little longer. And then a cold breeze that reminds you of winter rushes through them. Those leaves start dropping down, and you know all of a sudden that the day and the summer are over."

Raymona listened and turned her thumb down.

That week, Matthew's massage clients noticed not just earnestness in his voice, but also a shudder of urgency. As he ushered them to the door leading to the outside world, he would say, "You know, I'm going on a trip to the Boundary Waters next week. I'm really excited." Then he would look down. "This guy named Dan is picking me up Monday morning."

CHAPTER 9

Like some coliseum virgin with her eyes raised to heaven while being circled by a lion, Matthew waited for the big morning. And then the moment came. As birds began complaining in the dim light, he got up, dressed, and deposited his pile of bags at the down stair's door; he walked back up to wait for Dan. They would then rendezvous with Arnie and James Arndt.

He sat up on that porch of his, looking out into the gray, no sparkles in the night sky, just the cold quiet moment. Then his face snapped into alert as he saw Dan's van sneak up in that morning.

Matthew rushed downstairs, swung the door open and took a quick but more public look at his gentleman caller's face. "Oh Dan, it's so good to see you." Matthew wanted to be friendly, but not to friendly; after all Dan was married, sort of. Still Matthew noticed how Dan the Man, like some great white hunter, hoisted Matthew's bulging sack to his shoulders. "Thanks Dan. I'll get the rest and lock up. It's really nice that you're picking me up."

Dan's face cracked into a little smile; for a second his eyes glowed like coals that somehow made it through the night. Trixie eyed her master carefully from a van window.

The two voyagers stepped into that van, a boys dream: canteens, lanterns, a tent, hunting knives, compasses. State Park stickers from across the country decorated the windshield with memories. The engine churned up and was running; the driver resolute.

Dan had a way of keeping his attention fastened to the road; no chatty conversations that could lead to wrong turns or even worse, getting lost. It's not that he wasn't friendly, but he was doing this determined, resourceful, silent, male thing. No unnecessary familiarity here; that's for people who need reassurance or even worse are actually afraid.

Despite the privilege of having that male paragon sitting next to him, Matthew couldn't help but notice that it didn't look like a promising morning. It was the kind of gray that stiffens fingers and makes shoulders hunch up...cold. The chilling wind blew, trapped restlessly under the steel lid of clouds. They would be heading north, way north.

Dan scratched through the silence. "So you've got all the things you need?"

"I sure hope so." Matthew glanced at him and then back at the unpromising morning. He really did hope so.

"We're old pros at this...aren't we Trixie?

She wagged her tail desperately.

"It was really nice of you to lend me that stuff. So you go camping a lot?"

"Well," Dan jerked his shoulders with boyish modesty, "I go out every chance I can get." For the first time he gave a sideways glance to his passenger; a smile brushed Dan's face.

This gave Matthew a little permission to look at his driver again. Matthew noticed how tight the skin was pulled across the bones of that intrepid face, as if that tightness could seal in any feeling that wanted to sneak out. For a moment Matthew was brushed by something unnamable, a funny feeling that it wasn't just Dan the Man sitting next to him, but a breathing person who also didn't like to get up early, someone who was sitting there noticing things, someone who maybe even felt... who knows what.

Matthew even glanced at himself in the rearview mirror. Mornings demand cold stark attention. Then with a sigh of resignation and forgetfulness he inflated his world with stories about Dan the Man.

Dan turned to Matthew for a moment almost like he wanted to say something, then turned his head back to the road to find his solitary track again. The van stopped at a red light. "Next summer I want to go ocean kayaking in Australia."

"Kayaking, wow, is that hard?" They slipped into a more comfortable rhythm.

"Well you have to keep your balance just right, but I've been doing it for years...never done it on the ocean though."

"That sounds exciting!"

Even Trixie got up from her seat and wagged her tail.

In silence the van drove up Arnie's gravelly driveway. Arnie lived in an old part of town that was cut off from the rest of the city by a loop of the Mississippi River. In that neighborhood, the more conservative 1950's were maintaining a successful defense against both urban decay and 1990's chic. Small manicured lawns were fenced in like castles. Kids with slicked down hair followed their more formally dressed parents to Sunday Mass. Occasional statues of The Blessed Virgin Mary enshrined in bathtubs dotted those quiet streets. Some part of Eastern Europe had been magically planted in the Midwest...a lot of Catholic churches, but very few Goldbergs or Washingtons.

Arnie's house was pulling his reluctant neighborhood into the nostalgia of the psychedelic 1960's. Purple trim, leggy flowers planted in the front yard instead of grass, and tie dyed curtains peeking from the windows; all tugged annoyingly at the other more conservative houses.

Now Arnie's house shone like yellow beacon on that murky morning. Dan lead the way inside where Arnie was frantically scurrying from pile to towering pile of sacks, making sure that everything was there. "So you guys made it. Thought you'd stand me up."

Dan gave a smile and a tired wink.

Matthew nuzzled into the kitchen behind him. "Arnie, can I do anything for you?"

Arnie looked up with the irritation of someone who

was being delayed from doing everything all at the same time. "Where's James Arndt? Oh ya, thanks. Why don't you make yourself at home, be it ever so humble."

Dan looked up from a chair that he had slid into. "Where's Lance this morning."

"You know husbands, never there when you need them. He's on one of those fairy weekends...construction boots and chiffon, you know Lance." Arnie and Dan threw a complicit look back and forth.

With satisfaction Matthew realized that he actually knew who Lance was, Arnie's partner. Armed with that little sense of self accomplishment he shuffled around the house like he actually might belong there, but somehow no matter how many pictures he looked at or how many windows he stared out of, he still didn't have anything to do, and he felt he should be doing something. There was Dan; there was Arnie and finally there was this cold unpromising morning in which he was alone. Matthew walked out the back door of the house.

Someone with a sense of humor would have appreciated the friction of two stories rubbing together, but this was hardly an option for Matthew. Instead, he struggled briefly, wondering where he had gone wrong. Why he was standing in the backyard of someone he barely knew at 8 am on Sunday morning.

This was one of those times Matthew tried to forget...when he was in the boundary between things. He couldn't see a likely story, and he never had relied much on his powers of self reflection. No story here, just a black hole into which everything disappeared.

He jolted himself awake, and then once again felt for the gentle tug of a current, for that splendid pull that would wipe his memory clear of everything except for that shining promise of a new story.

If Matthew were home, he would have pulled himself together and sorted through one of those paper bags of old letters. Or even better, he would have called Raymona and asked her how she was doing. She would crunch on popcorn and then he would start picking at the thread of another story. Both of them would feel safe again. "You know Raymona, for a moment today I had this strange feeling, like maybe nothing's worth anything, do you know Raymona? It doesn't even matter how many trips are ahead. Then it was all over like a bad dream. Funny isn't it, like a dream...You wouldn't believe who I ran into yesterday."

Measured footfalls on gravel interrupted Matthew's reverie; James Arndt was walking up the driveway. On each third step, he methodically sipped what looked like coffee from a white paper cup. Perfect method impelled him towards Matthew.

"Hi James Arndt."

James Arndt's eyes nodded up from the paper cup, and coffee carefully slid down his throat. "Is Dan here yet?"

"Ya, he picked me up."

"Aren't you the lucky one…"

Matthew followed James Arndt into the house.

When James Arndt enters a scene, whatever should happen, usually did. They got into the house just in time to see Arnie stretching out his arms as if to calm the multitudes. "Well chappies, we're all set. Let's get this show on the road!"

Arnie, Dan, and James Arndt began grabbing bundles and oars and sacks with the design and premeditation of ants. Matthew shuffled his feet for a minute and then fell in step, scrambling to imitate their sense of destiny.

They trailed back and forth between the house and van, the piles in the house transformed to one large pile in the van. As automatically as they started, they ended; the task was completed. Dan began arranging the supplies in the back of his van, while Arnie, and James Arndt carefully tied the canoes to the top. Matthew again bereft of destiny, wondered around looking helpful and trying not to look like he hoped to sit up front with Dan.

While fastening a canoe with one last tug, Arnie yelled, "Hey Matty, do you miss your mother or something? Hop in. You can sit up front; James Arndt and I'll sit in back. We're going to check out a new route on the map."

At last...everything was tied or packed, and they all sat in their seats and closed the doors behind with a banging finality...done and ready for take off. Dan turned the key of the ignition, the van started rumbling and then it spun off that gravel driveway towards the Boundary Waters. For a moment each face in that van was caught in silence, eyes curiously emptied into that mysterious boundary between here and there.

Fortunately James Arndt brought them back from that dangerous edge. "Last Saturday morning, early, Theodore and I had finished jogging. We were eating breakfast at The Egg and I. We had just sat down and ordered the fat free vegetarian omelet, when who did we see across the room trying to hide from our view, but Roger and Mac. No one goes to The Egg and I on a Saturday morning early, unless they have slept together the night before."

Arnie's eyebrows shot up.

Barely taking his attention off the road, Dan smirked. "Now boys, maybe they were networking. They're both lawyers."

James Arndt joined in more sedately. "Why Mac, I certainly enjoy your back door communication style, so determined and penetrating."

Even Trixie was getting excited, wagging and panting and making little pleading, moaning sounds.

Now, humor wasn't Matthew's strong point. Humor implies some kind of friction between two stories that nudges people for a moment into a little bottomless gap where they fall through and feel tickled.

Matthew uneasily broke through the conversation. "Well you guys sure seem to know a lot of people."

Silence filled the car. Finally Dan looked over at Matthew for a second. Inadvertently, their eyes met. Dan's quizzical glance edged into a protective smile. "They're these two guys who went camping with us a couple of years ago. They didn't know each other before the trip. They were such pains in the ass, fighting with each other constantly."

Arnie exploded into laughter. "Pains in the ass? I didn't know any of that was going on."

"Oh, they were difficult to be with." Matthew nodded his head as if he had a sudden revelation.

The rollicking humor deflated into silence. Matthew shifted his weight uneasily. The wheels whirred on the freeway; Dan stared straight ahead into the tunnel of his thoughts. Occasionally he would startle, nudged out of his dream. Then he would suddenly glance into the rear view mirror as if he were afraid something was following him.

James Arndt pulled out a book from his ever present briefcase and began methodically reading. Arnie he curled up in resignation on that car seat and fell asleep.

What a relief. Matthew felt that he and Dan were sealed off in this bubble of privacy, no more names that he should be familiar with, no more things he needed to say when everybody started laughing. No, he was just sitting in the front of a van with a big old gray sky hanging in front of him. Even better he was sitting next to a guy who a couple of years ago was beyond the reach of even a casual hello. "Hey Dan?"

Dan, like a sentry posted at night, nodded his head in the general direction of his passenger.

That was enough for Matthew. "You know, I remember seeing you at a contra dance a few years ago. It was Valentines Day."

Still looking ahead, Dan's face opened into a quick, secret joke of a smile. "That seems like forever ago. I used to go to all those dances. I was a regular dancing fool. I don't go so much anymore."

Matthew felt that uneasy friction between stories again: the story about Dan the powerful, great white hunter; and the story about an emaciated man who limped along with fear peaking out of his face. As much as Matthew enjoyed fixing other peoples' dilemmas, Dan seemed too immense and mysterious to figure out, let alone actually understand. Anyone who has all those state park stickers on his van must surely know where he's going.

Arnie must have had some sort of alarm that let him know when anybody in the vicinity was dipping into the blues. His voice rang out from the back seat. "Is everybody having fun? Let's stop at that pie place past Duluth a few miles, where we went last year."

James Arndt rose to the occasion. "I hope that you do not mean the place where Theodore found the worm in his blue berry pie."

Arnie started to make ambulance siren sounds. "Alzheimer's alert, Alzheimer's alert. That unfortunate tragedy happened two years ago. The pies at the place beyond Duluth are strictly vegetarian."

Matthew could almost feel the slimy mush of a worm in his mouth all coated in sweet blueberry. "That must have been horrible! You know I suppose things like that do happen. I once found a toe nail in a tuna hot dish. What did he do when he found the worm?"

There was another one of those stalled silences, like Matthew had driven the conversation off the road.

Finally Arnie stepped in. "He saved it for fishing."

But somehow no one wanted to talk anymore. Matthew knew that he had said something wrong again. It simply didn't occur to him that there were stories out there that may have little to do with him. In the past years he had managed to surround himself with people who were temporarily charmed or at least entertained by his preoccupying tales of high adventure.

Around 1 p.m. they pulled up to Betsy's World of Pies, a little house just off the highway with a large picture of a piece of pie mounted on the top of a ten foot post.

They all stepped out of the van. The cold nibbled on Matthew's fingers and was slipping down his sweat shirt. Dan raced towards the outdoor restroom. "I'll meet you guys inside. Trixie may have something to do out here."

The other three rushed into that little house where waitresses who would soon be coeds when the school year started again. They could cast off those aprons so old fashioned that even their mothers' would be embarrassed to wear them. Aproned, friendly, and robust in their hopes for the future they greeted their middle aged guests. "Welcome to Betsy's, home of the best pies in the world! What can I get you today?" Her smiling, young face stared down at each guest. "And what would you like today, sir?" She said the word "sir" with both respect and sympathy; after all she was temporarily protected from them by a chasm of age.

Dan opened the door letting in the gray wind that smelled of cold. The lace curtains on very clean windows trembled until the smell of hot pie stilled them. He pulled a chair out from the table, seated himself, and breathlessly rode that chair up to the table of his companions.

That was the signal, they all began ordering from the smiling waitress.

Matthew pulled his chair a little closer too. "So you guys were here last year?"

James Arndt was studying the menu, picking out the perfect culinary investment.

Arnie took a quick look at Dan. "I hope you and Trixie got everything worked out."

"Ya, right after she squatted and left a nice firm brown turd, she mentioned that she can't stand your deodorant...for my part, I haven't had a solid movement in years." Dan smiled, unconvincingly, but cavalierly at the eccentricities of his bowels.

The smile was an all clear sign for Arnie. He started revving up. "Sure Dan, tell us all the gory details, like whether you had peanuts the night before."

Matthew was suddenly on a humor alert. Dan who really did seem to be having difficulty with his bowel movements needed to be protected from ridicule. Matthew would skillfully change the focus from Dan to peanuts. He surprised himself and dredged up a joke from grade school. "Hey you guys, how do you tell the gender of candy bars?"

Puzzled glances ricochet between the other three.

"The one with nuts is male. Do you get it?"

After a long, empty moment Arnie returned the shot. "This is going to be a long trip." James Arndt touched up his neat hair. "Who invited him along?"

Matthew joined in the laughter unsure if laughter was the price to pay for membership or if some how he had made another mistake.

Fortunately the smiling waitress was now standing at Matthew's right elbow with a huge tray of pies. For a moment her face puckered as if challenged by some test for which she needed to get the best grade. "Let's see. The blueberry pie goes here, the apple here, the blackberry here, and that's right, the banana cream here." Her face relaxed and spread into a proud smile that waited for a grade or at least recognition.

But each of the four was already indulging in the privacy of their appetites. Attention constricted to pie size, they missed their chance to encourage the waitress. Matthew devoured his blueberry pie. That's when he noticed James Arndt; everyone except James Arndt had finished their pieces. Matthew found his attention drawn unwillingly but inexorably to his methodical companion's pie eating discipline.

James Arndt stared at his pie with concentration and then rested the side of his fork gently against a precise section of that crusty project. With the exact amount of force he needed, he broke through the top crust with a sideways stroke, then carefully slid through the soft blackberries with a mounting ecstasy and finally with one last burst of excitement broke through the bottom barrier of crust making a subtle but climactic clinging sound as his fork struck the plate. After savoring the experience, James Arndt shifted his grip on the fork to a more relaxed position and exquisitely skewered the carefully separated piece and raised it to his mouth which now had opened in invitation. Once the morsel of dessert was safely deposited in his mouth, his lips sealed off the entrance to prevent any unseemly escape.

Dan and Arnie suddenly needed to check double check the knots tying the canoes to the van, leaving Matthew to be the only witness.

By the time they all got back into the van, the clouds had lowered even more ominously and were raging across the sky; it was cold. Even Trixie peered at Dan, tongue imploring with wet apprehension. The van churned its wheels in the sandy parking lot and again they set their gaze to the north.

The road followed the shoreline of Lake Superior for miles as the pounding waves shot white foam high up into the air. The lake was like the back of some ferocious beast, heaving restlessly as if it were preparing to mount up and obliterate the day. A wind funneled through the narrowing space between sky and lake, desperately squeezing through.

Matthew hated cold; anyone who knew him understood this. Something about cold contracts stories and turns them into complaints. Stories need warmth to expand. Complaints...they were for chilly, reluctant mornings.

Matthew sat staring out into the frigid turbulence, occasionally smiling at a name bouncing around in the car that was beginning to sound vaguely familiar. If he had been home on a day like this, he would have turned on the heat, then given Raymona a call to talk about some new person he met or wanted to meet. Once again his stories would rise and expand around both of them. But marooned in this van, he couldn't. Dan's eyes silently staring ahead and the alien conversation rollicking behind, Matthew sat abandoned between things, in an empty space.

His placid smile hid the jolts of free falling confusion that he spun into, no markers for stories here, just something ringing, panicked inside, some warning that he was at the edge of his world.

The four stopped and walked into the ranger's station to get their permit. The ranger flicked on the movie about the regulations of the Boundary Waters; they traveled on.

They four hardly spoke as they stepped out of the van and tromped with their backpacks through the howling evening that had already started to darken. This was some kind of resort with four bunkhouses and a substantial looking house all lit up. They walked to their bunk house and opened the screen door meant to keep out mosquitoes, not cold...each voyager picked out a naked bunk. Even Trixie looked uncertain. This would be their last night of shelter.

They walked to that well-lit house; the first floor was a dining room crowded with tables and expensive souvenirs. Each souvenir manufactured in China proudly welcomed them to the Boundary Waters.

Matthew heard voices at other tables murmuring as they were finishing their dinners. Those voices never actually said that they were going into the Boundary Waters. They would simply talk about "going in," as if finally there was really only one place that you could "go in" to, and that place didn't have a name.

The four sat at the wooden table with a red plaid plastic table cloth. Arnie made a few half hearted attempts to entertain everyone, and then conversation was ground down by the sound of the wind scraping against the windows; the chill even penetrating the sullen moose head hanging above the table. When the waiter said that they were already out of this evening's special, something called Wilderness Walleye, "fresh from the lake and lightly breaded with Corn Flakes and crushed almonds in a piquant sauce of cream of mushroom soup," Matthew shuttered.

As the wind poked through the knotty pine siding, he focused on the table next to him for reassurance. There sat a father in a new, crisp sweatshirt emblazoned with "Welcome to The Boundary Waters, Gateway to Adventure." The shirt was already stained with a glob of bloody Hamburger. A vigilant mother with very tight curls of intense brown that seemed to squeeze her head in apprehension, stared intensely out the window. A teenage daughter listlessly picked at that last precious, unappreciated piece of Wilderness Walleye while dreaming of some boy back home. A younger boy looked suspiciously up at his father...was that disappointment? All seemed caught in amber like so many prehistoric mosquitoes.

The family's spirits were finally freed when the father picked up the check and studied it disapprovingly. His wife peeked over at it too; those brown curls tightened even more tensely. Then on cue they all stood up and filed over to the cashier and solemnly ventured into the night. They were "going in" tomorrow.

Finally dinners were placed in front of the voyagers. They resolutely and quietly picked up their silverware and began clinking and chewing.

Twenty minutes later, Matthew noticed that between careful bites, James Arndt was appraising the waiter with an eye of a connoisseur.

Arnie noticed his glance too. "Hey I wonder if we have room for five?"

Dan stopped staring at his empty plate. "Talk about a body that doesn't quit."

One of Matthew's empty smiles covered across his face.

Then Arnie muttered, "Eye candy, just eye candy."

James Arndt continued to methodically chew on the cud of his fantasy. "I'll give him a BIG tip."

Dan looked up again. "That's not what I hear."

Arnie started laughing and then quickly swallowed it. "Well gang, I have a special surprise for all of you. It's for our last night in The Boundary Waters, if you're all good campers and we're very lucky, you'll get to see what it is. But I can't tell you… it is a surprise."

Dan and James Arndt barely looked up. Matthew who didn't have enough hope left to imagine an end to the trip, grabbed the last dinner roll and swished it around in the cold juices of his North Woods Lumber Jack Meatloaf. The tolerant roll even picked up those little pearly hard blisters of white fat that had beaded up and coagulated on his plate. After all Matthew was "going in" tomorrow too. Finally they stepped out into a night that turned their words into cold, smoky clouds.

CHAPTER 10

1,500 hundred miles away from that northern Minnesota resort, Raymona stirred. No matter how loud she turned the radio and television, she couldn't forget that Matthew wouldn't, couldn't call her for a week, a whole week. Who knows what can happen in a week. Unlike Matthew, Raymona was aware that nature is full of idiots, people who grab at a bait and end out one themselves, devoured. Idiots always get caught by wanting something. That's why she kept attachments to a minimum, but try as she would, something always sat out there that couldn't be avoided. Before she knew it, she had to buy stamps or pick up eggs, or even worse deposit checks. As soon as she pared one thing down, something else popped up. She even kept trying to figure out some way to avoid her gynecologist. No matter how hard she tried, something from the outside always penetrated.

Love, love was the most invasive story of them all. Whatever it was beating inside that convinced people they loved somebody wasn't for her. She sat on the edge of nothing, alone, or at least as alone as she could manage. This was for Matthew's sake also. She needed to be separate, after all they were a bigger target together.

She could see them both plummeting down. After some momentary apprehension, Matthew would look over to her. "You know Raymona, do you think this blue shirt matches my pants? I don't normally wear blue, you know. You look frightened, can I do anything?"... splat! The splat part wasn't so bad, but she would have lost her concentration on herself. Those last moments of her life would be stuck in Matthew's story, and she knew how his stories kept going on and on. They would be entangled forever

She sank further into her old brown stuffed chair, a relic from her life in suburban Tarry Town. Despite all the padding closing in around her, her radio's heavy beating base of rap rhythm pounded through her. She didn't notice her whole body starting to rock to that primeval beat. Eyes closed, she began chanting, weaving intricate rhythms and rhymes, anything, anything to keep herself occupied, to prevent her from hearing her own heart pounding in panic.

CHAPTER 11

That next morning in the Boundary Waters, the clouds had vanished, revealing a sky that once again glittered with anticipation. The grass sparkled with tiny seeds of sunshine that left wet marks on the voyagers' shoes as they walked to breakfast, quietly, as if silence could keep those shoes dry. This was a serious day. Even Arnie's face was still, as if planning some delicate strategy. This was the day they would "go in."

This was also the second day of the adventure. Though Matthew loved trips, he was a two-day kind of person. Usually, in fact invariably, by the second day the trip would have reached its finale; he would already be trying to think of ways to describe his amazement to Raymona. But now on the second day, he was just starting, no end in sight.

The voyagers entered the restaurant. Heartened by the prospect of another meal, James Arndt took up his role as arbiter of good taste. "I saw Jonathon last week. He told me, quite off the record, that he is breaking up with Brad. Who would ever want to date someone with the name 'Brad.' It is an aborted sound not a real name, something you stick into upholstery."

The smell of coffee silenced him. They sat down at the plaid covered table. Even the waiter seemed especially solicitous; after all this was their last meal, at least there last meal before "going in," and after you go in, well who knows... A mild sense of urgency impelled James Arndt as he carefully ambushed little perfect squares of egg with his fork and whole wheat butterless toast.

As Matthew swallowed each bite of spongy pancake, it seemed to topple down from some immense height into the dark restless pool that had been his stomach.

Even Arnie, eagle scout Arnie, seemed nervous. He kept periodically muttering, "Well gang, are we all ready? Eat up, there won't be any cute waiters out there, only bears."

Dan's eyes barely flickered as if this journey were only a prelude for him. The other, real journey loomed just beyond his imagination.

As they finished breakfast, Arnie tried to prop up their spirits. "Wait till you see that little surprise I've planned for you guys at the end of the trip!" Matthew managed to smile as he folded his napkin.

Bud, a large man who reigned over this resort with a sunburned face and a smile as bland as cottage cheese, was waiting for them by the van; everyone piled in, except this time Bud drove...he was dropping them off. After miles of driving down a road so narrow that leaves flopped against windows, green and soft whooshing;

finally the van stopped in a clearing. The four stepped out placing their sacks and bags and canoes on a patch of dry crispy August grass next to a dark barrier of woods with nowhere on the other side.

Bud said, "See you in five days." Trixie's ears squared off, glancing from Dan to the departing van and then back again until the vehicle was out of sight.

Arnie snapped into motion. His attention began bouncing around like a flea on a hot frying pan. "Well buckaroos, here we go. Don't worry, I hardly ever loose anybody." His eyebrows bounced up and down. "I'll carry one of the canoes on this portage. James Arndt, you're looking butch this morning, why don't you take the other canoe. We don't want to scare Matthew away before he cooks supper tomorrow night. As for Dan, we're saving him to carry a canoe on the really long portage. We have a lot of stuff; we'll need to make two trips."

Then silently, like make-believe, the four picked up their burdens and moved into the shadow of the forest, the canoes in the lead sliding upside down through the damp shadowed tree trunks, single file. Even the birds quieted, leaving the soft padding sound of feet on the rocky path and a delicate dripping sound that seemed to come from everywhere. The soil here coated the rocks in a slippery membrane occasionally oozing into dark puddles. The dense but spindly trees clung desperately to that fragile soil. Their soft leafy canopy glowed green on the faces of the voyagers. Ferns arched like shadowy fountains across the path; here and there scattered more deeply in the gloom, patches of moss crawled over stumps like a living emerald glow...the sun and sky only a memory here.

No matter which way Matthew looked, everything was incomprehensible...no lilac bushes, no houses or even telephone poles, nothing to remind himself of his past life, that past so fertile in stories.

They padded up dark stony hills and into softer gullies, feet grasping like claws to the slippery path, trying to avoid pools so black that the bottoms seemed like wishful thinking. Their feet, as they attempted to detour around the dangers squished and mucked, leaving foot prints that filled with the seductive blackness.

For a moment a ragged patch of sunlight cracked through the glowing green and reminded Matthew of the sky.

Then he spotted it, a dazzle of yellow up ahead. Their steps quickened to the flame, closer and closer until the brilliant sky exploded around them with crashing light. Matthew's eyes shut to the overwhelming glitter and then gingerly squinted open to a crack.

He was surrounded by blue out of which light was exploding, bouncing back and forth between sky and glittering lake. The green soft tunnel that had been their world was now a shadowy past. Despite the shattering brilliance, soft lumpy dirigible clouds floated across the blue unharmed, leaving behind reassuring lapping sounds and the faint smell of fish.

They dropped their loads in the startling, brilliant chaos. For a moment even James Arndt looked surprised; his lips that usually pressed against each other unrelentingly, relaxed; and that funny little furrow between his eyelids disappeared with hardly a trace. That's when he noticed a tiny, soft green caterpillar that had landed on him in the woods. His lips pressed together with vigilant determination as he carefully flicked that creature away with a snap of his fingers, leaving his jacket unstained.

Matthew watched that little green caterpillar curl as it was snapped into unexpected flight.

With hardly a word the four retreated back into the dark woods to retrieve the rest of their supplies. Dan lagged behind; occasionally Trixie would spurt up ahead and then as if she had a guilty conscience, she would pause, turn around, give her master an apologetic glance before barreling back to his side. His face was frozen in secret effort as his breath tore through the liquid gloom.

The four finally deposited all their sacks and equipment across that portage and into the light. Dan lay back against a large sunny rock, his chest heaving up and down. James Arndt was methodically examining his shirt for any unwanted passengers. Before they could catch their breaths, Arnie pulled out a plastic sheathed map and crackled it open. "In case anybody cares, here's where we are." With a screwing motion he landed his finger on the map, at the edge of a little curvy speck of blue. "We have five days and six more portages. There's a nice campsite on the other side of this lake. We should get there by this afternoon. We could set up camp, spend the night, and start again tomorrow morning. I'm sure you'll all be glad to know I cook tonight. He grabbed a large canvas sack with "lunch first day" scrawled across the front and began searching the contents like it was a grab bag.

Matthew studied the map looking for hints of an ending. He spied Dan out of the corner of his eye, breathing hard and desperate.

The voyagers each rustled through the bag picking out hunks of cheese, jagged pieces of bread, and clumps of raisons all squished together. Arnie passed around a canteen of water from the bunkhouse tap, their last tap water. Matthew took an interest in the far side of the lake which allowed him not to listen to the story of some guy three years ago that forgot to bring his deodorant.

Finally everything was again resealed in plastic or canvas, the blue was waiting for them. Arnie took charge. "Let's get this show on the road. Dan and James Arndt why don't you guys go together. Matthew can come in my canoe. I'll show him the ropes." He laughed and winked at Matthew who managed to smile.

They gently placed the frail looking shells of the canoes on the water that glittered like broken glass. A northwest wind wobbled the empty canoe while Dan and James Arndt loaded their supplies. Each sack they placed into the canoe seemed to reassure it; the canoe settle more comfortably into the water. Then they waded out, first Dan and then James Arndt. The canoe bucked a little as each stepped in. Now they sat motionless in place and the canoe waited docile and purposeful underneath them. Dan and James Arndt dipped their paddles into the lake and like magic that frail leaf of canoe smoothed out like a torpedo and sliced into the waves leaving a silent "V" of a wake.

"Now Matty my boy, it's our turn. Once you're in the canoe you have to keep very low and not make any sudden moves. The paddling is pretty simple. The person in front keeps going like this." He took a paddle in both hands, pushing it back to his right side. "The person in back, paddles and steers. He looked at Matthew.

"Ya?" Matthew, a nervous question mark, nodded.

"You'll see, it's a snap, anybody can do it. I'll steer this first time and show you how it's done."

Matthew waded out already starting to crouch down as if the sooner he bent over the more likely his chances of dry safety. At first the canoe attempted to spring away as he stuck his first foot in. Then with an impulsive act of faith, he shifted his entire crouching body and found himself bobbling in the canoe. He gingerly sat down on the wooden plank of a seat. Arnie slipped in; the canoe shuddered and sank a little deeper; it needled out into the lake truer than time.

Matthew began swinging his paddle imitating Arnie's motion. At first his strokes were tentative, barely reaching the water. Then with a burst of energy his paddle sank down so deep that he almost capsized the boat. Finally almost by accident, he caught a rhythm; the muscles smoothed out over his shoulders, and his arms dipped with a steady pulse. The canoe sped out faster into the lake, and he, Matthew Pierson was part of the cause.

The cool air off the water rushed moistly across his face, not like a story all contained within a beginning and an end, but rather a streaming of wind and water with Matthew in the boundary between. The water thumped against the front of the canoe as if its heart was beating.

They followed the other canoe around a gray rock of an island; around the shore of that island, low lying grasses waved like the water surrounding them. Blueberry bushes beginning to turn autumn red crawled up the rock toward a pine tree secured in a large crevice at the shattered peak. The spiky needles of the pine combed the rushing wind; Matthew could hear sighs of contentment.

The lead canoe now shifted toward the left and began sliding up a tail of the lake that twisted toward the east. Arnie and Matthew followed the curving wake. The wind stopped spraying into Matthew's face and caught the canoe from behind and pushed. Arnie kept the course true.

The shore of the lake began narrowing on either side. Alders and white birch began seductively dipping into the water like sirens. The front canoe drew to the shore. Arnie and Matthew followed slicing through whipping bull rushes that whispered against the sides of the canoe. They glided to the edge of a large flat rock that stuck up a few inches above the water. Rusty patches of lichens scabbed the gray, wave sprayed surface.

Both canoes sidled up to the rock; Matthew stuck out his paddle to prevent the canoe's outer skin from scraping the rough surface, and then he grabbed an edge of the rock with fumbling hands and pulled the canoe near. As all four stepped on to shore, the canoes lost their purpose and once again became fragile shells at the mercy of the waves.

James Arndt was already standing composed on the shore. "Is this where we stopped last year and John almost fell into the lake?" He clucked his tongue.

Arnie looked up from the corpse of the canoe at his feet. "Who's idea was it to bring him along?"

James Arndt smiled at him in accusation, narrowing his pristine blue eyes.

Arnie shook his upper torso like a wet dog. "Oh yeah, it was my idea wasn't it? You HAVE to remind me about that, don't you. I forgot you keep a ledger. You're the only person I know who can travel for five days in the outback and still smell like his mother's closet."

They eyed each other like two sumo wrestlers, and then broke off into tight smiles.

Dan looked up briefly while dropping brown tablets into a large plastic jug holding cloudy lake water.

The cool northwest wind began picking through Matthew's damp clothes; he sidled up to Dan, inconspicuously. "Dan, what's that for."

Dan looked up with the elaborate patience of a boy scout who was earning his badge. "Do you remember a few days ago when James Arndt was talking about the guardia in the lakes up here? Well these little pills take care of that problem. They're iodine tablets. You drop a tablet into a container of lake water, give it a minute to dissolve, and presto...drinking water. Even so we're careful to get the water from deeper out where it's colder. Guardia don't like the cold." He turned his attention from that plastic jug and Matthew. Dan's voice suddenly took on tones of intimate tenderness, his eyes dropped to his furry companion. "They don't like the cold, do they Trixie. They're not tough like us." As Trixie's tail revved up to a frenzy of wagging, Matthew began silently wondering which sack held his jacket.

All around Matthew the three others began moving rapidly with mysterious purpose, as if guided by some deep, inner camping instinct: tents went up, a sack of cooking utensils spilled out on a flat topped boulder, lines of rope were strung between trees, and finally a camping stove was placed on a picnic table. Matthew watched the rapid tide of sacks moving from the beached canoes to a circle of bald ground, in the middle of which sat a heavy rusted metal grate that crowned a ring of boulders. He tried to discover a rhyme or reason to that powerful tide. "Oh, can I give you a hand with that?" or "Gee maybe you'd like me to do that?" Each time he was swept further up the shore of his embarrassment. Finally unable to even look busy he came up to Arnie. "Looks like you guys know what you're really doing."

Arnie had thrown one end of a rope over a high pine branch, and now was hoisting the ponderous pendulum of a food sack ten feet into the air, hopefully high enough to be out of reach of bears. Straining and puffing he grunted.

Arnie hissed. "Be careful, stand back!"

Contrite, but determined, Matthew tried again. "You know, why don't you let me help you?"

"No, I'm okay, just move BACK a little!"

Matthew scrambled back almost falling into a large bush. He waited there like some child deposited by a parent. Finally the large sack tied and gently swinging over their heads, Matthew mustered his familiarity and approached Arnie again. "You know Arnie, I'm not sure what to do to help you guys. You all seem so busy doing what you have to do..." He left his sentence hanging up in the air like that load hanging above them.

Arnie tensed. "Well, why don't you wander in the woods for a while and look for dead branches for the fire tonight." His frown edged into a relenting smile. "Watch out for the bears now Matty."

Matthew set out into the wilderness. He had even found his jacket. The wind had picked up smearing shadows over the late afternoon. A few clouds raced frantically across the sky fleeing the coming cold of night; a fire sounded like a good idea.

Matthew stepped cautiously into the woods, each step deepened the leafy screen around him and his companions. For the first time in two days he was almost alone; even the familiar laughter of his three companions seemed like the sound of a television in the next room. Invisible, he breathed more deeply.

He wrapped himself in the shadows and stood there listening in his secret place.

James Arndt's voice clipped in, "Who's sleeping with whom tonight?"

Matthew indulged in his hiddenness and listened.

Arnie took up the challenge. "Now everybody can't sleep with me, so who would your second choice be?"

Matthew decided to walk deeper in the woods; there would be more branches there.

He followed a path leading towards the out house. An evening wind was stirring the green above him, and the glow was fading from inside the woods. Something brushed across his left knee, a plant peeked out of the shadow, its two leaves all soft and floppy. At a kind of crotch where the stems of the leaves joined to the thin green trunk, were a pair of translucent ruby like berries. This was clearly a creature of the shade. The leaves spread out like large delicate membranous hands collecting the sparse light, and the berries were cushions of red, watery blisters untouched by a drying sun. Before Matthew stepped off the path to look for dry wood he gently stroked the trembling leaves finally resting the lightest tip of his fingers on the red bubbled berries.

Then he remembered those voices on the other side of the woods and began reaching for broken branches, placing the jagged pieces in his arms. When his arms were full of that rough burden he started back in the direction of camp. The padding sounds of his foot falls were soon replaced by the ricocheting voices up ahead. Right before he entered that charmed circle he began to make conspicuous, crunching footsteps so that they would be aware of his presence. The conversation stopped.

Arnie was making supper; James Arndt and Dan retreated to their tent. As James Arndt zipped the tent open with precise determination and crawled in with Dan the Man in tow.

"So there you are Matty, my boy." Arnie's voice nudged through the sound of air mattresses being blown up in the far off forbidden land of Dan's tent.

An innocent smile spread like a mask over Matthew's face.

Arnie glanced up at him and then began burying his attention in clattering pans. "You're going to sleep in my tent tonight. Why don't you set up your air mattress and sleeping bag?" He fixed his eyes on Matthew with just a hint of pleading. "Okay?"

"Ya sure Arnie." The once brilliant lake was now a cold disappointment, grey metallic waves banging against the shore, the sun of Dan's warmth set behind his canvas tent walls. At least nobody knew Matthew's hopes, especially Arnie. No stories here, only silent complaints. The cold wind licked the tip of his nose. Wrapping his arms around himself he retreated to Arnie's tent zipping it open and slipping into a small world, dimly lit and flimsy around him. The sound of crickets filtered through the smell of canvas, a semipermeable private place.

He sat in that flimsy membrane of a tent. One minute the voices outside would startle him with their presence, and the next moment some inner private voice would nudge him. Both were happening at the same time, and he was on the boundary between them.

Things were actually going on out there beyond the canvas membrane. People were talking about some fantastic character with his own name, an actor in their story. Matthew was part of their story, how strange, like there were two of him, one here, one there. He stirred and unzipped the flap of the tent to enter a world without knowing which person he was supposed to be.

Out there a fire crackled in a frustrated attempt to dispel the chilly gloom. With relief he noticed that the saturating darkness would prevent anyone from seeing the craziness in his eyes. Only less vulnerable prominence like cheek bones and foreheads were burnished in the orange light of the fire. The dark bushes all around were grinding with cricket sounds. As the other three moved with light hearted precision, Matthew experimented with stepping toward the burnishing fire and then back into the cricketty darkness. Now you see me, now you don't.

Supper consisted of metallic packets. Arnie dumped them into water boiling mercilessly; the gas burners hissed blue.

The darkness was now complete. The sky didn't waste any light except for the cool chips of stars that kept getting sharper, the colder Matthew's fingers became. The wind stopped; the cold was here to stay. The four filled up their bowels twice; first with something called North Woods Stew, and then with Campfire Cheese

Cake. Almost before finishing the camp fire began fading until only embers winking and disappearing.

Arnie's voice broke through those last crackles of light. "Are any of you kidlets scared?" The fire popped and for a moment flared up. Trixie's head bounced up, ears squared off. She shot a concerned look at Dan and then, reassured, relaxed with a sigh. Arnie took center stage. Dan and James Arndt became absolutely silent; some first night camping ritual was about to begin. Arnie's voice cackled with exaggerated menace, eyes now black holes. Then there was a long pause filled with cricket sounds and suspense. Arnie was ready. "I talked with Steven yesterday. He's started dying his hair, not that he actually told me. Some people talk about the weather or their latest romance, not Steven, he lets you know about the latest tragedy. With that pale skin of his and that dyed black hair, he's straight out of a vampire novel. There in the middle of Walgreens, next to the toothpaste, he began talking about a cousin of his, Rosemarie. I was just minding my own business, looking for dental floss.

'Steven put one hand on his hip and started leaning on the denture powder shelf. I knew I was in for it.

'It seems years ago his cousin, Rosemarie, married a rock band promoter named Saul. They traveled all around the country meeting rap singers and young women singing about love lost. Rosemarie and Saul loved their life and each other. She gave birth to a son whom he insisted on calling Luck. After all they were very hip and lucky.

'Blessed by fortune, the three prospered. A few years later they found themselves in Phoenix, Saul was checking out a Latino band called Zapata. Rosemarie and Luck stayed behind at their motel. She was reading WOMEN WHO RUN WITH WOLVES, and young Luck was swimming in the pool with inflatable water wings that their clients from Orlando, The Fallen Angels, routinely passed out to all their fans.

'A perfect day, the wind blowing warm on her face, she slipped into a comfortable moment of sleep. Then she woke up and noticed the water wings floating in the pool. Boys! They never pick up after themselves. She called out, "Luck, Luck come out here and put your water wings away, right now!" Her voice echoed through that brilliant afternoon, but something inside her head began ringing. "Luck, Luck, where are you?"

'WOMEN WHO RUN WITH WOLVES fell onto the turquoise colored cement. She jumped off the lawn chair and ran into the motel room. She couldn't look towards the water. The room was quiet except for the reassuring sound of the air conditioner. Her hands automatically tore at her face. Now she could only hear the ringing inside her head as a voice outside herself started screaming through her mouth. She ran out to the pool and mechanically looked back and forth across it as the siren voice screamed through her lips. Then the siren stopped as her eyes fell on a little dark shape pressed against a corner of the pool at the deep end.

'As people crowded around her, her mind fell into that dark, deep shape."

Arnie's voice disappeared into the night with a sizzling sound. The voyagers fell into the darkness of the Boundary Waters. The fire was dead and crickets chanted regrets...if only I had, if only I had, if only I had.

"Come on Arnie, get real; how did you know all that stuff...WOMEN WHO DANCE WITH WOLVES.... I hope this wasn't your big surprise. Like I really need to hear about some little kid drowning." Dan's voice complained out of the dark. "Is there supposed to be some sort of moral or something to all this?"

James Arndt began making clucking sounds from the other side of the cold fire. "How about you can never count on luck."

Matthew wanted to play too. "You know, how about, never wing it alone."

They were laughing, they were actually laughing at Matthew's joke! He was on stage in the middle, that's where he was. Then the laughing stopped as if something were wrong. The shuffling sounds spread out from the dark circle, then a high pitched zipping ripped through the night...Dan had gone to bed. The others followed suite.

Matthew crawled in first, then Arnie. Both slipped into their sleeping bags; the high pitched whisper of bodies rubbing against cold rayon filled the tent. The lining of Matthew's sleeping bag was so cold it felt wet. "Good night Arnie, thanks for tonight."

The night called out, "Goodnight Matty." They both slipped into that shadowy hole on the deep end of the pool.

Suddenly Matthew startled awake. The crickets were silent. There was no light or sound except for the gravelly breathing next to him. His feet felt shivery cold as if they were resting on ice cubes, and yes, oh yes, he had to pee so badly that it was going to tear out of him in a sharp burst. He blinked his eyes in the darkness to try to focus on his familiar bedroom window. All he could see was darkness...any hope of the familiar caved in around him...he was camping, camping in The Boundary Waters. That breathing was Arnie. Pee, he had to pee.

After the darkness was named, a voice inside from some hidden corner of himself said, "You can go out and pee, it won't be so bad." He found his shoes; his icy feet touched the cold soles of his boots. His hand found the frigid metal tent zipper and he slithered it down. Icy air rushed in and dowsed him. He stepped out, and the sky opened deep like some bottomless hole into which he could fall if he didn't hold on to the tent. There were stars; they hung at various dizzy depths, shiny cold markers into vertigo. He stood up and shoved his head up among those points of light. Some stars were so close they almost burned his face like hot ice; others shone faintly so far away that he couldn't look at them or he would tumble into the depth.

Something scurried across a leaf nearby and anchored him to land. A distant "O" from an owl repeated, the lake lapped in chilly rhythm. Shivering started rumbling from deep inside his body. He clenched his teeth to prevent his head from shattering off into frozen bits of ice.

He stopped on the outskirts of the clearing and pushed his wildly jerking hand to another cold zipper and reached to the warm secret of his cock, like a robin pulling out an unwilling worm. He blinked once just to make sure he actually was awake and standing outside, then released the knives in his bladder. The stream of liquid rushing against leaves joined the other sounds of The Boundary Waters; his teeth unclenched, self splattering into the night.

He coalesced around the last determined thrusts of urine, and fled trembling back to the tent. Finally his sleeping bag once more enclosed his body spasming like some restless larva.

CHAPTER 12

He woke to light seeping through his eyelids and birds chattering. Curled in his sleeping bag he heard the tent zipper rasp open and Arnie step outside. Matthew's eyes burst wide as he heard the tent zip shut and Arnie's steps shuffled toward the out house.

Then there was sounds of clattering pans. The zipper of the other tent opened. Urgent steps pushed out fleeing to the out house.

Arnie's voice caught that refugee. "I thought you'd never get up; I've already milked the cows and washed three loads of laundry while you two were getting your beauty rest."

Dan's voice edged open. "You're gonna make some man a good wife, Arnie."

Other steps exited more serenely from that tent. James Arndt's voice modulated a clear note. "I need my sleep Arnie, I'm not a natural beauty like you."

Laughter bounced around the camp.

Matthew wanted to stay hidden, but someone might mention his name. He slipped out of the sleeping bag and into his shoes and clothes peeking out onto blue sky with green leaves stirring in a sunny surprise of warmth.

"Talking about sleeping beauty, look who's up." Arnie glanced over, his face creasing into a smile as he poured water into a pan. James Arndt lit the hissing stove.

Matthew just knew that he was supposed to say something funny. All he could think of was, "How did you guys sleep?"

James Arndt picked up the sagging question. "I usually sleep lying down Matthew, how else would I sleep?"

The three others laughed.

Matthew tried to join in with the laughter. If only he could laugh, everything would be all right. He took a plunge into comradeship. "I was cold last night. My feet never did warm up. It was kind of scary for a while."

Arnie kept clattering pans, and James Arndt began fishing out metallic envelopes. Dan relented for a moment and looked at Matthew. "When I got up earlier this morning to pee, there was frost on the ground. Must have got below freezing. Trixie was shivering until I called her into my sleeping bag."

Arnie's voice called out. "Poor Trixie, she'll never become an eagle scout."

Preparation for the meal continued with mysterious precision.

About midway through breakfast, Dan's face tensed up and he fled to the outhouse again. Arnie covered his retreat by collecting dishes as loudly as possible.

Matthew and James Arndt were left sitting on a log, the morning twinkling across the lake.

"How was your night James Arndt?"

"James Arndt's lips unsealed. "I cannot complain."

Matthew felt the warmth of the log beneath him; he continued. "I got scared last night for a while. You know it was so cold. After I got up to pee, I couldn't stop shivering. Were you cold last night?"

James Arndt sat with lips sealed shut. Despite the soft smell of morning rising around him, his thin face tightened into a very precise, stony cringe. "I do not know what we are supposed to do about that, Matthew. This is just the beginning of the trip. I hope you do not want to go back."

Matthew rebounded, perplexed. Then some new urgency to explore the unknown propelled Matthew outward. After all he had three days of this trip a head of him; he needed to do something. "You know James Arndt, I just can't seem to find a way to talk with you guys. I don't understand what's going on."

James Arndt's face began cracking, frustration hissing out. "I don't know what you mean. This trip isn't a consciousness raising group. What are you trying to do?" With some effort, his face was once again quiescent. "I have to go floss my teeth. We are going to depart soon."

Matthew sat there. Something warmed inside him and strangely he was just there. Nothing else mattered. How strange to simply feel the sun toasting his face and smell the sweetness of ground warming. His eyes noticed a single bird sailing silently across the lake. The bird dipped down. No story at all, something else.

It's time to brush his teeth…he crawled in to the open flapped tent, and sat next to his backpack resting quietly in a corner of the tent. Back to the entrance his hand searched through the few remaining objects from his former life. He heard Arnie quietly slip into the tent.

"Well Matey, are you ready for the long one?" Arnie leaned over Matthew with comic menace.

Matthew's eyes expanded. Somewhere between wonder and panic, he smelled the peanut butter on Arnie's breath. "The long one?"

Arnie interrupted Matthew's squirming. "This'll be the longest portage of trip today. It'll separate the men from the boys."

Matthew's mind fled in panic, leaving his face limp behind."

"You betcha! But don't worry, I'll be there. You better get your things ready."

The four dipped paddles into the lake, waves touching the sides of the canoes with gentle patting sounds. They were off for their second day in the Boundary Waters. The daunting portage ahead sat like a weight in Matthew's stomach, drawing the sights and sounds and smells and feeling in towards its cold mass. There was no place to hide; there was only that semi-permeable privacy, separateness after the worst came true with Janes Arendt.

The canoes knifed across the lake. Their pathways sealed up again as if they had never troubled the water.

Matthew and Arnie took the lead today; after a minute of instruction, Matthew steered in back. Arnie pointed in the general direction and Matthew was to keep the craft on a bee line. With tensed arms he started paddling with frantic exactitude; he jerked his head up frequently as if he were trying to follow a specific, unforgiving course. The slightest deviation propelled him to increasingly frenzied effort. The canoe would lurch from right to left in frantic compensation. While a wisp of cloud was slowly passing over head, hardly leaving a shadow, fatigue and some inner learning gradually straightened that jagged course into a smoother approximation. Probability was enough to keep the course.

As sparks of sunlight flickered off across the endless surface of the lake, Arnie called to Matthew from in front. "Do you see that beach up ahead just to the left of the bunch of tall pine trees?"

Matthew squinted his eyes along the shore, and then his face opened up in excitement. He found it. "Ya, I see it Arnie!"

"Now Matty, easy does it. Steer in along the left side of the beach."

The canoe hooked toward the destination. The shore opened up like a cave all around them and scraped the bottom of their craft. Jumping onto the sand they slid the canoe up to the lip of the woods.

The longest portage of the trip stared at them out of the dark woods. Perhaps Matthew was drunk with the triumph of steering the canoe, or else he just wanted to prove something to those guys. "I'll carry a canoe; it's my turn." Without waiting for any kind of an answer, he grabbed a canoe by its up-side-down empty belly, tightened his grasp and shifted his weight swinging the canoe backwards and up. Suddenly like a miracle, the canoe was sailing above his head.

The four set off on the portage, Matthew in the rear. Matthew's feet danced around keeping balance, as the canoe settled on his shoulders. His head nestled in the belly of the canoe, private from the three others. His eyes focused on his shoes, occasionally tipping the canoe up like a visor to see ahead. He set out, drawn to the dark pathway that reached out ahead of him.

Occasionally if he turned a corner too fast; the canoe would hit a tree, tolling like a deep resonant bell around his head. Sometimes his feet would start sliding towards a black pool, and then he would dance to find solid ground. He was sailing, even if it was up side down. The craft was biting into his shoulders and gonging his head, but he kept moving ahead into the shadowy woods.

And he noticed things in that narrowed, downward field of vision. A tiny orchid with a blossom that glowed like the moon was tucked into a rotting tree stump. A wild blackberry bush frantically reaching up to escape the darkness snapped at his bare arm. Those low bushes he had seen before with floppy leaves and soft, ruby fruit peeked out at him from the half light.

Up ahead he heard voices crackling. Matthew tipped his visor up; yellow light shone out of an opening in the gloom. The longest portage was finished, and he had carried a canoe!

"And here comes Matty, approaching the finish line taking up the rear."

Matthew looked up and smiled, triumph still echoing in his head. He shouldered the canoe down and retreated to the edge of the shadow.

James Arndt had already stationed himself on a sunny boulder, his pale skin glistening and rosy with exertion. "Do you remember when George wanted to turn around and go home after the second day?"

Arnie accepted the challenge. "You can't blame me for that one James Arndt. Dan was the one who picked that rare jewel to come along."

Dan too was in the shadow, air rasping in and out of his nose and mouth. Even though his face looked toward the lake, all his attention was concentrated on those rapid breaths that he didn't want other people to notice. With frightened eyes he stored up a deep breath and then said as casually as he could, "You gotta admit he was cute."

Arnie broke out in a frenzy of scampering laughter to cover Dan's desperate trail. Matthew watched.

After a few minutes the four headed back into the woods to get the rest of the sacks. Matthew and Dan lagged behind and entered the woods together; even Trixie was up ahead with the two others.

"Matthew what happened to your hand?"

Matthew stopped, surprised to hear Dan say his name. His body flushed dizzily, and for a moment he didn't care about anything else but the sound of his name on Dan's lips. The woods, the Boundary Waters, James Arndt...nothing mattered except Dan's voice. Matthew turned his head toward that voice. Just barely ahead of Matthew, Dan's eyes stared out from the shadow, soft like stars on a warm, humid night.

Matthew's arm, his arm, he drew his eyes away from Dan's radiance and looked at his own arm as if it belonged to someone else. A line of red slashed down the outer side and ended in a curve by Matthew's wrist. For a second it looked beautiful, like the bud of some strange long, soft flower beginning to open. He remembered the desperate blackberry bush snapping at him. "Oh I must have scraped it against something. It's not bad at all. It'll be alright." Matthew looked back at Dan apologetically. Then for the briefest moment, much against Matthew's better judgment, he lost himself in the depth of Dan's eyes.

Matthew fell into those eyes that now shifted like two huge kaleidoscopes, holding hopes and fears and dreams all changing shapes and turning around a still spot in the center that was this moment. He and Dan were looking at each other straight on. Dan saw him. After all, that was Matthew's hand, Matthew's body that Dan noticed.

Then it was over. With a little embarrassment, Matthew crawled out of those eyes and looked down to the ground.

Dan caught Matthew's embarrassment and smiled quietly; Matthew glanced up. Their eyes entangled in a moment beyond space and time, not heaven really; there's still a connection to time in heaven. Then both began struggling against that unrelenting tenderness; back to designs and names and futures and strained forgetfulness.

In a gallant farewell, Dan reached over and gently lifted Matthew's hand, the blood still blossoming on his wrist. Dan's face bowed, his lips parted, "Can I kiss it?"

Matthew lifted his hand, and felt the fleshy moth wings of Dan's lips flutter against his wrist.

Just at that moment Trixie came bounding back to check on her master. Dan dropped Matthew's hand. "You worried about me Trixie, you worried about me? I'm all right, such a good dog. Thought I forgot about you didn't you."

Trixie's whole back end wagged with pleasure; she gave out a little squeal. She had captured Dan's attention so thoroughly that he appeared to have forgotten his other companion.

In fact if it weren't for the lingering feel of those dry fluttery lips on his hand and the sting of that long red scratch, Matthew would have wondered if it was all a dream.

Dan and Trixie set out to join their other companions. Matthew followed, occasionally looking from his wrist to Dan and back again, wondering. His attention was jerked to the sound of laughter ahead where sun was breaking through the half light. "So there you guys are." Arnie grabbed the sack labeled "lunch." "It's about time for lunch. We have a long day ahead and we don't want to loose anybody."

Through his composure, James Arndt shot a sharp glance at Matthew and stationed himself next to Dan. "Well, I'm certainly glad that there's been no problem so far. Do you remember when Larry starting lagging behind all the time?"

In that clear light of day, Dan stroked Trixie and joined in the laughter. Matthew remained in the half light.

The voyagers ate their pieces of cheese and bread salvaged from the lunch sack, and then set off again in their canoes; the blue shimmered all around them, earth and sky barely bounded. Arnie steered while Matthew paddled in a quiet rhythm, a rhythm that reassured him. The sympathetic tapping of waves against the canoe joined with the beating of his heart.

They camped that afternoon on a bare point of land fingering out into the lake, the warmer air of daytime barely budged from the boundary Waters that evening. It was Matthew's turn to cook. The night before he had watched Arnie's moves as he made supper, flashing pans and mixing packets in boiling water.

He sidled up to Arnie. "Hey Arnie, you know it's my night to cook. Maybe you'd show me how to use those gas burners and where pans and utensils are?"

Arnie's face became serious, almost solemn; he fastened his eyes on Matthew as if he were imparting directions for an arcane mystery.

Matthew tried to look impressed.

"Now Matty, any time you work with gas, you need to be very, very careful. Who knows what could happen. First you take the stove out of this box, then place it on a level surface." As Arnie spoke the sacred words, his hands were demonstrating the ritual. "Then you pump this handle a few times, take matches out of this special packet, turn on this knob, and light the burner. Then you turn the flame down with this knob. You look into this sack for the pans. You go over here and get the utensils out of this bag. And finally you let the bear proofing sack hanging in the tree, down and pull out the sack labeled "Matthew's Supper."

Matthew watched Arnie moving around the camp with the formality of a high priest. With each word was a gesture and wala! an act was accomplished. Suddenly supper was in motion around Matthew, boiling.

"You see Matty, there it's all done. It wasn't so hard, was it?"

Matthew nodded not so much with gratitude as relief. Even though the mystery prevailed, all he had to do now was stir. And he kept stirring. In fifteen minutes as the aromas of something called Lakeside Lasagna and Pine Tree Pudding were wafting through the evening air, he found himself surrounded by his comrades. The four shoveled the food into their bowls.

James Arndt began delicately picking at little strands of noodles as if each doughy strand had to pass some stringent test before it slid into its destination. "Do you remember when Richard made chow mein?."

Dan was beginning to examine the contents of his

bowel too. "His mother sure didn't teach him how to cook. I gave most of mine to Trixie. She's never forgiven me."

Trixie's ears cocked up; she gave a wary sideways glance to Dan, then she slumped down again, perhaps still upset about the chow mein.

James Arndt had filled the fire pit with sticks and logs woven into a precise mound; around the pit, careful piles of wood were also stationed around the pit. Arnie lit the masterpiece. A lone cricket chirped from behind the tents and ignited the evening into sound. From somewhere across the misting lake, a loon wailed, waiting for a response that never came. As if restrained by some unspoken law, they all waited as the tiny deliberate clatter of James Arndt's spoon and plate held their attention captive.

Matthew looked up at the sky. At first he thought he might be imagining a faint point of light in the fading east. He looked around the camp at his companions; what a day it had been. He looked up again; points of light WERE poking out all over the eastern half of sky, timid at first, but no longer just imagined.

James Arndt's had finished his supper. His pale face now hung...a phosphorescent moon over the camp site. His body sat in the shadow as if it had slipped between both day and night and for an instant, there were no rules to follow, no precise regimens. The man in the moon opened his mouth as if something inside were spilling out. "My mother was a Kitterbeck from

Dubuque, Iowa, one of the lovely Kitterbeck daughters, and the most intelligent."

Arnie's fidgeting ceased, and Dan looked at James Arndt with relief. Anchored in a familiar story, for the duration of that story he would be in a quiet harbor, protected from the open seas of his future.

"We Kitterbecks are an old family who lived on the bluff above the town, at least most of us did. Occasionally a Kitterbeck carelessly married into one of the, shall we say more dubious families, down by the river. Of course we always provided Christmas baskets for those unfortunates, after all they were still Kitterbecks.

'My mother, Julia, married an Arndt, a good family from a neighboring town, an acceptable marriage. Of course an Arndt is not a Kitterbeck, but it was at the beginning of the Second World War. When Vern Arndt came calling, his marine uniformed filled out with his husky body and fervent devotion to Julia, she did her patriotic duty. The Kitterbecks come from a long line of patriots.

'Though she needed to suffer the name, "Arndt," shortly after her marriage, as if in compensation, she became head librarian of the Kitterbeck Library. After all deep down inside she was still a Kitterbeck; blood runs true. When Vern was stationed over seas he left his loveliest Kitterbeck behind with a little Arndt planted in that sacred soil. I was born nine months later in Kitterbeck Mansion at the very top of the bluff, growing up with all those Kitterbecks...happy that I belonged.

'Then one day while I was playing with all my Kitterbeck cousins, a man knocked at the door. We little Kitterbecks peeked out of the window and saw his big face peppered with coarse black stubble that would surely pose a threat to softer Kitterbeck skin.

'My mother had not gone to work that day, but had kept cleaning out closets in a controlled frenzy. She ran to the door, opening it. Her face grew still, looking for something that she knew she would never find. She propped a smile on her face and turned to me and said, 'James, this is Vern Arndt, your father.' And then she stood there unmoving as if she had completed her duty to this stranger.

'Aren't you going to hug me Julie?' Vern looked like some stray dog begging for a home. Graciously her willowy, fair body extended itself in his direction to bestow an embrace. I could see her head perched in privacy over his shoulder...cool Kitterbeck eyes.

'The first thing that Vern Arndt did when he came home was to take us from Kitterbeck bluff and move us to Plattsberg. Everything was flat in Plattsberg, Arndts all around. That is when I found out that I was an Arndt. I can still hear my mother say, 'Now James, a real gentlemen makes the best of things, even if they are unpleasant. From now on you're James J. ARNDT.'

'I started school that year. The first day of class, Mary Jane Compton, one of my classmates in kindergarten, looked me up and down. 'Who are you? What are you doing here?'

'I thought that fine sounding name and the pink

dress she had on were indications of distinction. Very confidentially I said, 'My name is James J. Arndt, but actually I'm a Kitterbeck.'

'A Jitterbug?' She started laughing in a very unbecoming way and finally burst out, "Jimmy Jitterbug, Jimmy Jitterbug." First one and then another of those Podgorskys or Reillies called me Jimmy Jitterbug. It was very embarrassing, but as a gentleman, I made the best of it.

'Every week my family had to get together with the rest of the Arndts. Vern would usher my mother and I into that old ford of his that smelled of animal feed (Vern was an animal feed salesman). We would go to one of the Arndts' houses. All those Arndts would be drinking beer and laughing and talking about all the other Arndts. If it was summer, all the stocky, thickening Arndt men would take their shirts off and play football. I never saw so much sweat. Even worse, I was supposed to play in all that roughness. At least my mother only had to watch.

'At first Vern tried to teach me how to throw a ball, but he soon gave up. I heard him say to my mother, 'Your precious little James throws like a girl.' After that, whenever Vern took his shirt off, which he did at the drop of a hat especially when young female Arndts were around, I felt like throwing up.

'Julia faced trials too. All those Arndts would whisper that my mother was not a real woman, because she escaped the Arndts five days a week to the Kitterbeck Library in Dubuque...she worked.

'I got the best grades in my class, and sometimes as a reward for my performance Julia would wake me up on a school morning earlier than usual and say, 'James Arndt, today is a Kitterbeck day.' Then we would both head out to Kitterbeck library. While she would be busy cataloguing books, I would sit in the entry way under the bust of Trevelane Kitterbeck, my mother's philanthropic great uncle, and wait for people to notice the uncanny resemblance.

'Unfortunately things were not going well in Dubuque either. The post war housing boom was spreading common suburban houses all up Kitterbeck bluff. Kitterbeck mansion itself was sold and torn down to make way for BUNGALOWS. Old names did not mean anything anymore; Dubuque was becoming vulgar.

'My mother and I made the last heroic stand for quality at the Kitterbeck library. She would sit behind her desk, examining everyone who entered the library. If someone especially a child made noise, she would snap her pen precisely on her desk and fasten the young delinquent with a stare that made him wish he had never been born. As she used to say, 'There is never an excuse for being common.'"

James Arndt's face tightened and flattened like disk in the sky. He carefully dusted off his lap and proceeded to his tent, leaving the Boundary Waters to grieve the demise of the Kitterbecks.

CHAPTER 13

Warm air rested curling over The Boundary Waters that night. Matthew woke up to find his arms and shoulders exposed to the morning air; his torso was damp. Arnie still breathed with the innocence of sleep. There was an acrid odor of unwashed bodies in the tent. For a moment Matthew rested his eyes on that face next to him as it heaved with relaxed breaths, he rested his eyes there not to find cues or get instructions, but simply out of curiosity. The flaps of Arnie's nostrils open and closed; occasionally his lips would part, releasing a sigh of a breath, an overflow of comfort. After two days of not shaving, gray hairs stiffly poked out of Arnie's face pointing in all directions.

Arnie sniffed and scrunched up his nose as if he were trying to itch it with his upper lip. Under his eyelids, his eyes began jerking and rolling; irregular human grimaces began taking over that face that once rested at peace. Just as his eyes were getting ready to open, Matthew closed his and lay as still as he knew how. Perhaps at that moment Arnie began watching him.

Arnie got up first and left the tent; he had things to do. All clear, Matthew opened his eyes and stared at the glowing canvas, waiting for the sound of voices outside. Only then did he reluctantly stir in his slithery sleeping bag and get up to join his companions.

The third day, the third day of his trip. After today only one day left, and then he could return to his apartment, those bags of letters, and long distance Raymona.

And then like waking up he noticed In the morning warmth, smelling of pine and fish, and the baking the rocky soil. Thick, hot air enclosed the Boundary Waters.

A routine now, their days were becoming routine. Oatmeal, reminiscences about people Matthew didn't know, and finally setting off in the canoes. No breeze today. The lake was so still that frogs jumping into the glossy water resounded with a thump across the lake and set off fragile ripples that spread outward. Sometimes two frogs would jump into the lake at the same time. The waves would meet each other and then get mixed forming what seemed like a new and chaotic pattern. Matthew wondered about this and was sure that Raymona could explain the transformation. He was sure there was meaning in the chaotic ripples. The canoes silently slid into the lake, heat smoothing any illusion of disturbance on the surface.

A large "V" winged bird circled over head riding a dipping roller coaster of air over the lake. Then it plummeted downward with thrusting speed and nipped a ripple of water, sailing upward now with silver in its claws.

Looking down over the edge of the canoe, Matthew could see the ghostly lake bottom slide by, a world of dream hills below, covered with grass that waved as the canoe sailed above them. Then suddenly his eyes would tumble over the edge of a canyon, plunging into a cold darkness that even summer couldn't touch. In a haze they steered onto a shore with a black fringe of mud that buzzed with insects. Above the ooze a large boulder hung, massing the heat of the day. Orange lichen streaked down it's warm back like some beautiful skin disease.

Their shoes squished onto the steaming beach, sweat glazing each face in privacy. Arnie mopped his forehead with a red bandanna and tied it round his head. James Arndt merely glistened. Dan breathed ferociously in the hot, heavy air; he hardly spoke, but his eyes stared out glazed in private mysteries. Matthew took his blue canvas hat off, the rim was wet, sweat had seeped up the canvas leaving a salty irregular line. He wondered what he smelled like.

Once settled on shore, Arnie pulled out his trusty map from its plastic envelope; he glanced a little too casually at Dan's gray, straining face. "Well campers, I have a great idea; this is a short portage, and there's two campsites on the next lake. No sense in all of us sacheting around the lake to find the best camp. Why don't Dan and Matty stay right here, and James Arndt and I will go scout up ahead."

Dan struggled to smile, but only found breath enough to nod.

For the briefest of seconds, James Arndt's face scowled at Matthew. Then he too noticed Dan's heaving chest and responded to Arnie's call, picking up the canoe without a complaint.

Dan and Arnie exchanged a glance like some private sad melody that only they could hear. Arnie and James Arndt slipped into the woods, leaving their two companions on that beach.

Dan was already sitting, his breaths tearing through the afternoon quiet. Matthew paced, remembering yesterday's kiss in the half light, but now even that seemed like a flimsy dream next to Dan's desperate gasping. Matthew shrugged his shoulders in the broad day light and sat down next to Dan.

Time buzzed by in hazy warmth. A delicate flicking sound revved near Matthew's feet and focused his attention. A blue needle of a dragon fly gently rasped its wings in the still air and slowly descended in quiet jerks to the edge of a muddy footprint that he had left behind. There, the dragon fly landed and slowly spread its fragile, glassy wings. That blue needle of itself curled segment by segment in languorous delight. All the while light played through those outstretched wings; new colors shone through the veined transparency with each delicate movement. Then without any preparation, the dragon fly flicked into the air faster than a moment, wings again rasping away until the sound blurred and disappeared into the afternoon.

Matthew wondered why things so beautiful and hopeful could shine without even a hint of permanence. Even a small cloud passing overhead, could shadow and dim the brilliance of those wings as if it had never been. And if he tried to grab that dragon fly; he would be left with a wreckage of cellophane and crushed blue in his hand.

He looked more closely at that footstep that he had left behind in the black muck; lake water had secretly seeped in and now tiny creatures small as dust wiggled and crawled and spun through their tiny world, as if nothing could stay empty and disappointed long. The most casual loss fills with new worlds shining.

Dan's breathing had now softened. His face opened to the afternoon and Matthew sitting beside him.

Matthew felt Dan's attention the way a blind person feels the sun shining. "Hey Dan, look at all those funny little things squirming in that foot print."

Dan shifted his body towards Matthew and while the afternoon buzzed they watched side by side as those tiny creatures swam and mated and ate each other and died.

Grasses were rustling with sleepy afternoon stirrings, one lone bird call needled through the distance, something on the shore plopped into the lake, a dragonfly jerked on to that footprint once again; its wings casting rainbows.

"You know Dan, when I was a kid I loved to walk around the woods, looking under rocks just to see the way the ants made those funny burrows underneath.

Like it was my private world. It was all contained and safe, and all those ants seemed to know exactly what to do."

They both nodded together solemnly.

Then Dan looked over to Matthew, relaxed and easy as if nothing mattered except this afternoon and talking the way kids can sometimes. He smiled as if a memory appeared as suddenly as that dragon fly. "When I was a kid I lived next door to this old couple." His whole face opened up in that buzzing, hot afternoon. "The man said he was an entomologist. I think that was the biggest word I had ever heard; so I knew he must be pretty important. I asked him what that word meant. He looked at me for a minute and then very mysteriously went into his house. When he came out he had a silky net with a wooden handle. It was a summer evening and things were shadowy and cool. He walked out into the yard all silent and empty except for a few cricket sounds. WHOOSH! He scooped up some air down by the grass, and then we both sat on the front stoop to examine what he caught. With one hand he pushed up the bottom of the net so we could see what was in there. I couldn't believe it, there were hundreds of tiny winged, fantastic creatures all crawling at the bottom of the net, a whole menagerie all out of nothing. The neighbor looked me straight in the face and said, 'that's what I do.' Then he emptied the net out with a gentle shake so that all those creatures could return to that place that seemed so empty before. Right then and there I decided that I wanted to spend my life discovering all the creatures around me. I was pretty good at science anyway."

At the word "science," Matthew shifted uneasily. "I was never very good at science. I couldn't figure things out very well in school. I did pretty well at English though, but that didn't seem like something boys were supposed to be good at."

Dan didn't answer; his face had that far off haunted look again that didn't allow anyone near. Just like that dragon fly disappearing in an instant, the contentment of the afternoon vanished without a trace. Matthew looked down at the muck and only saw empty foot prints of his failures.

Matthew heard the telltale sound of steps through the woods. He looked up just in time to see Arnie's face poking out of the tall grass.

"Well scouts, what's up?" Arnie grinned.

Dan had found his more heroic self. "What's up? I was just waiting to see how long you pussies would take."

"Who are you calling a pussy?" Arnie put his dukes up and danced around in the muck, squishing and leaving foot prints that would soon become new worlds for little wriggling creatures.

Dan started laughing nonchalantly.

Then almost like clock work the four began picking up canoes and packs to set off.

The four set off on this next portage that snaked along a sunny marsh. Grasses crowded the path, sometimes obliterating it. Even though the path was level and dry, Matthew felt the ground tremble under each footfall, as if beneath the fragile membrane of soil, water lay listening to every sound, noticing each creature walking across it. Occasionally five foot clumps of grass would rise like green fountains out of the shorter grasses. All the while the sun coated the voyageurs with sweat.

Finally they slid the canoes into the next lake. Arnie and Matthew took the lead. Once on the water, afternoon light exploded in Matthew's eyes, even the birds were too hot to call out. The paddles dipped with syncopated automation and pushed the canoes across the slick surface of the lake, simply one paddle stroke after the other. Brilliant spangles were scattered in the wake of the canoes.

Matthew felt Arnie arc the canoe to the relief of a shadowy shore. The beach once again whispered and then scraped against the bottom of the canoe; they bounded out of that shell leaving it bobbling in the shallows. Matthew pulled it up on the beach without even wondering what he should be doing. The other canoe pulled up, Dan limped out rushing to the out house. The other three began carrying sacks up to a flat rise above the beach. Eyes still dazed with brilliance, Matthew realized that he was part of this camping ritual.

Dan stepped out of the woods to find the tents already up. "You guys are getting good at this; maybe I'll take you along next time."

Arnie took one last swing at a tent stake. "We just wanted to show you how real men set up a camp site."

"Real men, real men, that's not what I hear."

Suddenly Arnie began tearing off his clothes and running toward the shore. "Last one in the lake is a pussy!" He left a trail of clothes down to the beach. At the very brink of the water he bent down, pulled off his underwear, and swung them up in the air where they landed on an overhanging birch tree, a gray, yellowing flag of masculinity.

Dan took up the challenge, slipping out of the cocoon of his clothes, his body stretching in the warm sunlight.

Deliberately, maybe reluctantly Matthew began unbuttoning his shirt. Even though he would reveal the most intimate story at the least indication of interest, he didn't like people to see his private flesh, or for that matter, for him to see theirs. It wasn't a question of modesty. Deep down inside, and he could hardly admit it to himself, we all look the same, like disappointing plucked chickens. And disappointment, that was what Matthew feared most.

James Arndt was determined to disrobe genteelly. He walked behind some pine trees and after a few minutes squeezed out fresh and naked as a lily. The carrot colored hair around his groin opened to the air like the innards of a flower.

Matthew was afraid to look too closely, lest his eyes be smeared with orange pollen. Besides he had his own nudity to be concerned about...he was down to his underwear. He paused and looked out into the distance perhaps to prolong a last vestige of mystery.

There, there at the beach, Dan stood, set against

the shine of the lake, his darker form etched from sparkles. Matthew's eyes squinted and then tried to catch the substance of that body. Dan's flesh was draped, puckered and loose over shoulders that were still wide. Empty sacks of skin hung down from his backside, a memory of maleness waiting to be immersed by...there was a moment of solemn silence as that shriveling form slid into the setting sun and disappeared into glory.

"He was magnificent once."

Matthew turned to see James Arndt standing next to him looking out at Dan with wistful disappointment. Matthew's eyes still held the image of Dan walking into the brilliance; and he didn't want James Arndt to talk about Dan in the past, like some ruin or even worse...a story. Even with his eyes closed, Matthew could still see the light around Dan and feel the evening warmth. He wanted Dan to always be setting out for another wonderful trip, kayaking, or mountain climbing, or scuba diving. Most important, he didn't want Dan to ever be in the past.

James Arndt was now silently stepping into the lake, his pale body slicing into the water, perhaps not even getting wet.

Matthew dropped his underwear on the shore. As splashing and laughter jangled the air, he too edged slowly to the beach. The pebbles under his feet turned from hot and dry to moist and cool. In a tickling surprise, water licked between his toes. First his feet then his legs gradually disappeared into that silvery cool which finally reached up its icy hand and grabbed his genitals with shivery, shocking delight and pulled him down into its heart.

CHAPTER 14

The morning of their last full day in the Boundary Waters, Matthew again woke up to the glowing tent and the regular pulse of Arnie's breathing. Matthew closed his eyes as Arnie began stirring. Arnie zipped his way out of the tent leaving Matthew a few wide eyed moments of privacy. He stepped out into that morning smiling blankly at his companions; he knew that he didn't have any stories to match theirs.

He picked out a packet of instant oatmeal, tearing a corner off the brittle envelope rippled on the edges, pouring steaming water from an aluminum pan into his gravelly mixture.

"Do you remember how sunburned Ray turned last year, a ghastly shade of red; I told him to bring sun screen and where to get it." James Arndt voice stung like an enraged hornet.

"I thought he looked attractive, like a boiled lobster." Dan licked the oatmeal paste from his spoon.

Matthew smiled with a strange nonchalance.

"Well scouts, today's our last full day in the

Boundary Waters. If the sky stays clear tonight, wait until you see what I have prepared for you." Arnie waved a large serving spoon like some scepter of authority.

"We are not some of those campers you used to lead out into the wilderness." James Arndt admonished.

But Matthew had found an opening. "Arnie, is that what you used to do?"

There stretched a long moment of silence. Then Arnie made a grinding sound as if he were switching gears clumsily. "Well I used to." His face kept shifting, first humor, then sadness, then anger, then tenderness, and finally his face settled into sarcastic banter. "Every summer I'd pack them up and bring them out for a camping trip. I'd make sure that they all had insect spray rubbed into their little faces and at least two sets of clean underwear. They didn't understand why they needed TWO clean sets of underwear. I did."

Arnie pinched his nose and scrunched his face. "Even so I sometimes had to wash underwear by the end of the trip.

"I'd set out with all my little and not so little campers. "Arnie, Arnie why is water blue? Arnie, Arnie how come birds only sing in the day time. Arnie, Arnie if I go too far from the fire at night will a bear eat me? Arnie, Arnie...' One supper, I had just plopped down plates of my special spaghetti in front of their excited little faces. This girl named Maria looks at her plate and then looks up at me like it was the fourth of July. 'Arnie, Arnie, something real exciting happened to me today, just like my mommy said. I bled into my panties.

Like all of us wanted to hear about that, especially while eating spaghetti."

James Arndt was registering severe disapproval, "Disgusting!"

Matthew almost said, "You know that must have really been amazing for her to get her period and all," but he stopped. Instead thoughts rippled through that new private self of his, born in the tent these last mornings. He didn't need to ask anybody else, just to wonder.

Arnie's face kept shifting from a grimace to a smile and back again. "Well if you have to know, why I don't do it anymore. . .last year when I returned from camping with my munchkins, I got a pink slip with my check. My boss said that the funds for our department were being cut..." Arnie's voice just hung there for a moment gradually fading.

Dan covered over the naked moment. "Never trust anyone who gives you a pink slip...you might have to wear it."

"Pink is such a bad color for you anyway Arnie." James Arndt's voice edged into sympathy.

Matthew caught the wave. "You know Arnie, that sounds really hard."

"Hard? Who's hard?" Arnie reached towards his crotch. "We can't sit around here all day, we have things to do, scouts!" He started clanging pans and hustling around the camp, loose ends and regrets blurred in the commotion.

They packed up there camp, and set off this morning, the sky a clear, cool bell. The four dipped their paddles with precision; a light wind brushed their faces and gently thumped waves against their hollow canoes. They were looping back now towards the resort, one night still to go...and Arnie's surprise.

Matthew still hated camping, but when he thought of looping back, well he wasn't sure where back was anymore. The room full of letters, bemused clients waiting at his door, and the phone with Raymona on the other end; he could hardly remember them, or at least remember why they were so important. The important thing now was that he was steering the canoe, and he wasn't worried about it. The direction he was headed, the canoe, his arms, the cool air, the soft thumping water, his whole self...everything was together and speeding out into blue. Hoping and worrying had been replaced by a kind of itching, as if the Boundary Water were rushing through him, tickling him.

He felt the wooden seat pressing on his butt; up in the front of the canoe, Arnie motioned to swing towards the left. Such a confident and easy motion, his arm swinging through the blue and the canoe smoothly veering left...the intelligence of a single being. Arnie pointed to a bay with huge shattered boulders all around it. There at the very center of those rocks was a small muddy beach almost hidden by trees spilling out struggling to find soil. One stroke of a paddle and then another and another, in rhythm, the canoe closed in on the beach as easily as morning turns into afternoon.

Matthew didn't need words as he jumped out of the canoe and onto land. As the other three began talking about going bowling next week, Matthew placed his hands on the belly of the canoe and swung it up on his shoulders with a smooth curve. "Is this the right path across the portage Arnie?"

Arnie must have been feeling his own kind of simplicity. He didn't even grin but said, "Sure Matty, I'll follow you." The four filed into the woods. Matthew only gonged his canoe against a tree twice.

Once again they placed their canoes into the water... the dark water of a long narrow lake, a watery canyon shadowed between high walls of boulders. Arnie steered this time.

Aspen and twisty pine trees tried to find a foothold on those walls; any crack would do. The trees reached out horizontally from the steep jagged banks and then curved up toward the sky and sun. Matthew paddled and watched those trees. He could almost feeling them sending delicate roots down into the tiniest of cracks and then tenaciously holding on. No stories here, just the rhythm of heat and cold, dryness and moisture, and the reaching, always the reaching. As his arms and shoulders and whole body melted into their own rhythm, he felt that tickling again, something rushing through him.

The canoes veered to shore. Up a steep rocky path curving up from the shaded beach was a sunny shelf of land, a tiny plateau that stuck out from the tangle of trees. The platform opened out to the south, as if that whole end of the sky was an amphitheatre for viewing.

This was the last campsite, their last night under the

stars of the Boundary Waters...beyond this night was life as it had been, as if those stories that waited for the four travelers on the other side of tomorrow were the real life. Already Matthew could feel the subtle pull of his apartment, the phone, and most of all those excited hopes of his that were fixed like stars in his sky. Arnie and James Arndt began fixing their social calendars for weeks, maybe years in advance. Dan began separating more and more from the group, as if he were listening for something that was ready to spring out at him as soon as he left the protection of this trip.

A litany of lasts chanted through Matthew's head: the last time he would help Arnie set up the tent, the last supper by the campfire, the last time he would unzip the tent and crawl into his slithery sleeping bag, the last time he would pretend to be sleeping while Arnie got up, the last morning he would hear those names bouncing around outside the tent that he still couldn't get straight. The last, the last, his mind began flattening and stretching across beginnings and endings.

James Arndt, between unpacking pans and tonight's supper, fought to rest imperiled Dan's attention with more tales of hard won triumph in the crusade for quality.

Matthew flamed the coals of conversation, "You know, you guys, why don't I do dishes tonight?"

"That would be fine by me; I certainly do not want dish pan hands." James Arndt lifted his lily fingers to the side of his face and attempted to smile like a 1950's housewife struggling with the help of valium to maintain a spotless home and the freshness of eternal maidenhood.

"Imagine that face waiting for you at the end of day." Dan struggled weakly to take his part.

Arnie desperately stoked the excitement. "Never mind all that good house keeping stuff, doesn't anybody want to know my surprise?"

Only Trixie wagged her tail in excitement.

"Well if you'll all keep very quiet, I'll tell you. According to my handy almanac, tonight should be the start of meteor showers, and tonight's perfect. It's cloudless and dry and if you're good little boys and sit patiently looking towards the south you may be able to see meteors later." He turned his face up toward the sky and smiled with satisfaction.

Dan barely noticed the smile, he was too busy listening for whatever was coming out of tomorrow for him.

James Arndt began pulling the gas stove out of its box. "Theodore and I are going to Iowa next month."

Arnie grinned at Matthew with just a hint of desperation.

Matthew took the invitation. "A meteor shower, you know Arnie, I've never actually seen a meteor shower. That's great." If truth be known, Matthew wasn't actually THAT excited. True, he had noticed the night sky as it floated by his window on May evenings, and had felt something strange and sort of tender inside. That's when he'd call Raymona and tell her about his latest adventure; he'd feel better afterwards.

The sky stayed clear in the Boundary Waters that evening. While they were eating chicken cordon bleu and crepe suzettes that James Arndt had somehow created out of tin foil packets of freeze dried food, the eastern sky was turning an dark blue, and in the west the sun was slipping below the rim of the horizon. Between bites of supper the sun slipped and disappeared out of sight. Rose and green and purple began shimmering, marooned and ephemeral in the western sky, ghosts of colors shifting. The dark blue in the east began seeping across the sky absorbing those shifting colors until only the western edge of the sky shone faintly with the memory of the day. In the east, a tiny points of light punctured that dark ceiling and the sky became deep and endless, no boundary now. The solid world was transformed into dark flat shapes.

Point by point of light, the night opened out dizzily, falling further and further out as stars measured the depths with fierce precision. Some points waiting just at the edge of visibility, faded in and out, letting the campers know that no matter how deep that hole of a sky seemed, it was even deeper, falling into forever, and forever was too close.

The yellow tongues of the camp fire licked and snapped and pulled Matthew's attention protectively, establishing a frantic center for his world, giving flickering importance to the faces and selves of the voyagers surrounding it. All around them a stadium of crickets began cheering. For a moment Matthew wondered if his world was just a tiny dot of light in someone else's distance.

"There's one, over there, over there!" Arnie's shadowy form leapt up, the camp fire splashing light on that hand pointing to the sky. They each turned away from that security of the fire and looked out, their attention falling into the blackness. "Look there's another one, another one."

Matthew caught the second one out of the corner of his eye, a line of white streaking the sky, and then gone before he could believe he had actually seen it. Then, in full gaze, a meteor slashed the night. "Arnie I see it, I really see it!" Before he finished his last word another star fell.

Dan stood up quietly, sticking himself right up into all those falling stars and remained there motionless, his head tilted back like he was drinking it in.

The shadow of James Arndt began fidgeting, suddenly all composure was lost. His tightly modulated voice cracked open and out came something between a wail and a cheer. "There's another one. Just look at that. Can you believe it?"

The southern sky was now streaked with falling light. Matthew was frantic, trying to make a wish for every falling star, to not waste this opportunity for hope: here, this ones for Raymona that she gets out of her apartment and has lots of fun; here, this one's for his family that they all become happy and never get sick; here, this one's for Dan that he keeps scouting out wonderful adventures; here, this one's for Arnie that he finds someone to love him; here, this one's for James Arndt that he finds happiness on the other side of his crusade; here, this one's for everybody, that life opens out in wonderful ways; here, this one's for himself, that he learn to be really, really alive. And then even Matthew lost track of his hopes as stars kept sailing down... millions of messages from infinity showered the voyagers in wonder.

Even the moon cooperated that night and rose thin like the trace of a smile.

CHAPTER 15

Matthew opened his eyes to dawn; the tent walls were gray, beaded with moisture, and a wind outside kept gusting against the flimsy canvas, slapping it with cracking blows. Like a hangover, the gray chill of morning slapped his face, commanding him to wake up out of the memory of last night. Arnie's snores ground through the morning.

The Boundary Waters was finished with the voyagers. A cold, dark wind bore down from Canada pushing them out, the last morning. Matthew to squeeze his discomfort and apprehension into the format of a story, but it didn't work; something ran through him that resisted containment. He was permeable to the movement all around him.

Matthew shut his eyes as Arnie dressed and unzipped the tent to the punching wind. No matter how tightly Matthew curled into the shivery, clammy sleeping bag, he couldn't come up with a story. The only thing left was the funny churning in his belly that he hated and the sense of being cast down on this chilly ground;

afraid of people, afraid of being middle aged, and afraid of those body aches.

Then outside pans clinking against each other, boxes opening, waves churning against the shore, a few bird complaints, the unzipping of another tent, and Arnie's voice, "I thought you guys would never get up."

James Arndt's voice had a little crack in it, a little imperfection of phlegm marred his articulation. "This is not a good day for camping. How long is the trip back to the lodge?"

"Well I figure if we push, we should be back before evening. The wind is blowing some pretty rough weather in." Urgency edged into Arnie's voice.

The other tent unzipped again.

"There she is, Miss America...our ideal." Arnie's voice sang.

"Gotta shit quickly, I'll be back." Dan muttered.

"Thank you for sharing." James Arndt's voice followed him.

Matthew stopped staring at the canvas, slipped into his damp clothes, and unzipped himself out into the world of his companions. "Can I help you Arnie?"

"Thanks Matty, but we're all set. I think we better get an early start. Looks like rain."

As Matthew ate his oatmeal, he watched the gravel colored waves chop at the shore, threatening the flimsy canoes resting barely out of reach. Dan was back now; some urgency pushed them beyond bantering. Even James Arndt nicked at his oatmeal with type writer rapidity. While the chill seeped into hands and cooled the coffee, they ate silently glancing up at those low clouds churning not far above their heads.

The way out was gray, not only because of the sky and water, but because of their urgency to be somewhere else. Matthew and Arnie pushed out first, pointing into the cold wind that smashed against the canoe and drenched their faces with sharp cold drops of lake water, no rain yet.

Paddling, paddling, waves crushing against the front of the canoe, Matthew sat straining, looking out into the wetness as if the determination of his gaze would motor them through to the lodge. Matthew started imagining..."You know Raymona it was a really strange trip." A wave slapped his face, waking him up to the peril around him.

The canoe was jolted to the right. Matthew caught his balance and pointed his intent back into the wind. The sky kept getting lower; at any moment, thundering, the clouds would drop down and smash them.

Arnie veered the canoe towards a shore. They pushed into the relief of land, and in urgent harmony carried their supplies through the woods. Matthew heard rain begin striking the leaves above his head, at first the gentle sound of a few drops against delicate green membranes. Then the rain started bulleting down in a commotion of noise; the path turned into a stream of muddy water.

They reached the clearing and the broiling lake. Those lowering clouds pounced, slashing sharp cold drops into the voyagers faces. The four loaded the canoes under that pulsing attack, and slid out through the barrage of rain to cross another lake...no space for private hopes or fears.

Dan stopped wondering about his doctor's appointment next Monday; his breath strained and his arms numbed, he pushed across the lake. For a moment, Arnie didn't care if anyone loved him, he only wanted everyone to reach the next shore safely. James Arndt relinquished his brittle crusade for quality, his eyes pointed fiercely toward their simple destination. Matthew tasted the rain running down his face like tears and paddled, simply paddled.

They pushed to shore and jumped out of the canoes hardly noticing that their feet splashed into lake water. Arnie's hat was soaked, water funneling down the drooping brim; his hands were white. Coarse gingery hair curled out of his soaked sleeves and matted his wrists. Face set firmly; he looked at each of his charges, looking for signs of life.

Dan leaned against a tree, his chest heaved, rivulets of water ran down his ropy hair. He caught Arnie's eye and for a moment something unexpected opened out between them like rain from the sky, but softer, falling. Dan nodded. Arnie let his eyes rest on his friend for one more quiet moment. Then that moment too was lost in the flux.

"Well campers, last portage. You're doing great. We're almost there, just another couple hours. We'll make it. I told you I never lost anybody out here."

They all listened for a moment, no laughter or

stories, no need to even talk, they simply carried their burdens, and moved out. Trixie followed Dan, her hair clumped and wet, trotting along in line as if she were glad that everyone finally recognized the importance of what was going on.

As they placed their canoes in the last lake, the clouds began lifting. The distant shore of their destination became visible through the drizzle like a thin edge of shadow. Half way across...the air began turning from wet to dry-autumn-cold; the waves calmed. Subtly the four's shoulders began paddling at a slower pace, and one by one they started looking toward that final shore that signaled the end of their time in The Boundary Waters and the beginning of their more personal futures.

Up ahead looming closer every moment stood two dark masses of island, like sentinels between the voyagers and that final shore. Arnie steered the canoe toward the gap between; both canoes moved closer to each other and slid into that final passageway. Dark, blasted rocks towered above them on either side. All was silent in that narrow channel between those two dark walls, except for the sound of water dripping off rocks into the lake...a last syncopated rhythm from the Boundary Waters before they returned to that place where people believe in stories that tie lives up in hope and recrimination.

Matthew felt the tickling, almost a thrill, rushing through him in a wordless message. He turned around to Arnie who was solemnly gauging the glassy gap between the towering gates, carefully steering. For the briefest moment Matthew wondered why they had not become friends, then he turned around once again to paddle toward that thickening land ahead. He could just make out the rectangles of buildings etched into the shore.

Now they were released from the channel; the canoes moved easily toward the nearing destination. Before he knew it, Matthew's paddle touched the gravel of the final beach. It reminded him of the sound of popcorn crunching. He and Arnie gently scraped to shore and stepped silently out of the fragile craft that had carried them through the Boundary Waters. They didn't need words to know that it was over.

The canoes now grated against the gravel, and the four jumped out onto the shore. In the silent cold the campers unloaded the boats and carried their burdens to the familiar van. Somberly Dan placed every pack into the van like he was positioning things in a time capsule; he closed the back with a thud that sealed off the past. They all stood around the van. A bone cold night turned their faces into shadows, but there was no fire to be built or supper to made, even memories of past trips seemed stale or even worse, sad. The stars hid.

CHAPTER 16

"Raymona, you can pick up the phone. It's Matthew."

Raymona sat in her apartment; Matthew's plaintive voice filtered through her solitude. She took a deep breath, counted to ten, and turned the rap music on a little louder....she was ready. "How's it hangin' Matthew?"

"Hanging? Are you all right Raymona? I can hardly hear you, with all that yelling in the background."

"Of course I'm all right, just because you're away for a week, you think I don't have important things to do here? Besides, that's not yelling, that's my man Snoop Dog." She ground her heal into the floor.

"I know you have lots of really important things to do Raymona, but I couldn't hear you."

"When did you get back?"

"Oh, I got back the day before yesterday. How are you Raymona?"

"Don't try to change the subject, Matthew. You go away with Jack the Ripper and his buddies to a place with more fresh air than anybody can stand, and then you wait for thirty six hours to call me back...." She placed the telephone against the radio.

"Ya, I guess that is music Raymona." There was a long pause, as if Matthew was actually listening to the music.

Finally Raymona relented and put the phone next to her face. Matthew tell me all about your trip, everything..." She turned the radio down, her whole body shuddered melting into relaxation, and an expression of child-like wonder spread across her face. "I don't want to miss a thing."

"You know Raymona, it was the strangest trip I was ever on; not because it was dramatic or anything like that. Nothing really did happen, or maybe things happened but they didn't necessarily have anything to do with me. I was going over it in my mind, but it just doesn't seem to all fit together."

On the other end of the line, Raymona fidgeted. When has it ever been important for Matthew to find meaning? Insight had never been his strength, only luscious, dramatic repetition. She registered her complaint by turning up the music.

Matthew's voice strained on the other end of the line as if he were trying to force some kind of climax for his dissatisfied friend. "Well, I was going camping with these guys who I didn't really know. First there was the one guy I had a crush on a long time ago, and like I told you before, he's in the last stages of AIDS. He's still kind of wonderful but real skinny and has diarrhea a lot; he kept staring off into space like he was waiting for something, but it wasn't me. The other guys were kind of okay. One guy told jokes all the time, kind of like he had a constant itch, but instead of scratching he said funny things. But even with all that distracting stuff, he watched over all of us pretty well. The other guy was from this rich family, at least sort of rich for Iowa. He's an accountant; you know, the kind of guy who you tell something to and he tells you what list to put it on, helpful kind of but not real warm or anything.

'They were nice enough but they sometimes looked at me like my zipper was open. And they all kept talking about people I didn't know; I felt pretty stupid. We paddled and camped and paddled and camped. Sometimes it was cold and sometimes hot. Nothing on the trip had to do with me except there I was in the middle of it and I couldn't get out. And then one night meteors fell, and that didn't have anything to do with me either, except there I was, the sky so deep that there was no end and maybe no beginning either, but still the stars kept falling out of nowhere like there was no center to anything. It was really strange how it happened Raymona. Things didn't seem to matter to me so much after that"

Raymona nodded her head. "'Really strange tell me more, more."

"How are you doing Raymona?"

Her hand squeezed the phone so hard that she almost strangled it. He couldn't be finished, he couldn't. She had barely started listening. Disappointed but most of all shocked, all she could manage to say was a feeble, "Matthew...."

"Well Raymona, you know I better go to bed; it's been a hard week and all. I'll talk to you soon." She heard a gentle click and then an angry hornet buzzed into her ear.

What's happening? She knew that Matthew was at his most excited, story telling best when he was straining under a little sleep deprivation. And now he said goodbye after a mere nubbins of story, leaving her all alone to wonder if she had breast cancer or if her cat really was in heaven and what about her mother, not the Catholic one but the other one, her birth mother.

She didn't hear from Matthew for a whole week, not as much as a words. Finally, finally he called and innocently asked, "How are you Raymona?" as if she was the one who had the story to tell. "Matthew, how nice to hear from you. Hold on, I have another call coming in." Before Matthew could say, "That's really wonderful she had already placed the phone in a half empty tissue box and wrapped a towel around it. Then she finished watching the last twenty minutes of Bay Watch. Finally after the credits and during a commercial, she exhumed the receiver. "How's it hangin' Matthew?"

"Oh, pretty good," his voice was strung out a little more tentatively than usual.

She gave him a good two minutes of silence, plenty of time for him to start telling her what actually happened during the trip. She knew Matthew hated other people's silences and would automatically fill up that void with almost anything. Now the phone lay quiet and limp in Raymona's hand. Finally very matter of factly she said, "I've got an important call to make," and hung up in a very efficient and business like manner.

After that, he called her every week, testing the waters. "How ARE you Raymona?" Or, "How are YOU, Raymona?" Or even, "RAYMONA, how are you?" Finally during his last call, taunted beyond the endurance of a saint, she placed the phone with Matthew's tiny voice, in the toilet bowl just above the water line and flushed. She told him that a water pipe had just burst above her head, and that she had to run and get help before the parrot in the apartment below drowned. Matthew was alarmed.

It had been eight weeks now since he'd been back from that trip, and sometimes she didn't even bother to pick up her phone. That's when she discovered the "Jonah Game". She played the Jonah part, and the bathtub was the whale. She thanked Yahweh that her landlord had not remodeled the bathroom and replaced the deep claw-footed tub with a shower. The object of the game was to spend as much time underwater as possible, without dying.

That evening, deciding to play for the third time that day, she walked over to the bathroom, trying not to look in the mirror, and turned on the scratched hot water tap. It squealed and then started splashing water into the tub, crashing against the enamel; tiny, splattering drops cooling her skin. Even with her lack of trust she was am able to sustain the belief that that cold water would eventually become hot even if she left the room.

Next, she stepped out of the bathroom and kicked off her slippers. With a snap of her thumb, her blue jeans collapsed around her feet. Then she reached down to the bottom of her tee shirt and stretched her back a little too sensuously, pulling that shirt fragrant with the warmth of her body up and around her head. For a few precious moments her eyes, her face, her whole head were encased in cotton. Then she flung that shroud onto the floor next to her jeans.

With a serene face she delicately crossed her arms in front of her breasts in memory of all those innocents who had been torn to pieces by lions or Christians or slavers. Dropping her panties, she took a few steps to the tub and was swallowed up by the steamy mouth of the whale.

She settled into that stinging embrace and her whole being was seduced if not into pleasure, at least into some facsimile of safety. Her head broke the surface of the steaming water, gasping for breath...there, that was better. Her whole body in simple and drastic effort sucked in sweet air. Now her eyes stared out in a moment of peace. She could hear drips falling in a subtle rhythm...blop...blop...blop, setting the snaky wisps of steam to dance around her face and lick her hair. The water shimmered around her, winking light and sliding across her belly like a warm hand.

What WAS going on with Matthew? Maybe he had been hit on his head by a paddle during the trip and had lost his memory. Yes, that would make a good story. One glorious day he would call her up. "You know Raymona, I finally remember my name and what happened to me on that camping trip. It was so amazing, I have to tell you about it."

Oh my God, what if he has Alzheimer's disease, all those stories lost forever. Or even worse, what if he found God. Knowing Matthew, he'd do something drastic and preposterous like taking a vow of chastity, maybe becoming a nun. It would be a strict, intense sort of order. Once a year she, Raymona Washington Goldberg, would perform the ultimate sacrifice and leave her apartment to make a pilgrimage to Kentucky or Idaho, to that silent convent smelling of incense and mysticism. She'd knock on the huge wooden door with the tortured body of Jesus on it and be ushered into a small parlor by a ghostly figure in black. There she would wait in absolute, silent darkness until a little door slid open revealing a small latticed window. She'd see a shadowy familiar face straining against the screen.

"You know, Raymona, you wouldn't believe what happened to me last week!"

Very gently she'd say, "Try me."

Maybe she was a little hard on Matthew. Her reverie was interrupted by the ringing of the phone. Serenely she sat through the four rings and let it switch to voicemail. "Leave a message if you want to, see if I care." She waited for five desperate minutes before she listened to the message. "Raymona…answer the phone, you would never guess who called me Saturday?"

Raymona jumped out of the tub, shedding that whale like a bad dream; this sounded like the real thing. She slid across the wooden floor and picked up the phone, wet and naked as the day she was born. She listened to the message and called him. "NO, you don't say......"

She could hear a pause, as if Matthew were looking for the loose thread of a story, and patient person that she was, she waited, finally..."You know Raymona that Arnie guy from the camping trip..."

"Yeah, Jack the Ripper."

"Well, I was busy taping plastic to the insides of my windows, you know it gets so cold here, Raymona. I wasn't going to answer it. It's so funny Raymona, when the phone used to ring, no matter what I was doing, I just had to answer it. That call always seemed more important than what I was doing. What if something really exciting was going on and I'd miss it?

'You know Raymona, at least that's the way it was. But the funny thing is that lately, when the phone rings I jump but kind of get thrown back into where I am, almost like with a safety belt. Then I think, I don't need anything else going on; maybe I'll just finish this, even if it's something really boring like taping plastic up.

'So there I was standing on a chair, unrolling plastic and that phone just ringing away. I realize that I had left the scissors on the kitchen counter, so I decide to step down off my chair and get them; and on the way, I picked up the phone.

'Well it was that Arnie. He sounded all solemn

like there was hardly a wisecrack hiding anywhere. He said, 'Matty, I wanted to call you sooner, but I've been real busy. Dan got real sick and he only wanted me and Francis around. He said it was better that way. So Francis and I took care of him at the hospice and did most of the bathing and feeding. And then one day Dan decided that he didn't want to eat any more. Every time I put food by his mouth he'd shake his head, not desperately but just definitely, like he was preparing to go some place where he didn't need to eat.

A day after that, he motioned me over with his finger and then he whispered in my ear that he wanted to say goodbye to some people and wondered if I'd do it for him. I grabbed a piece of paper and started writing down names. He wanted me to say good bye to you, Matty. I wanted you to know that.'

'And Ramona I was so surprised, it's not like Dan had plans for me. I was just this goofy guy who had a crush on him. I know his saying goodbye didn't have to do with keeping hold of that. He was just saying goodbye to me like I'm really real, I wasn't just a story to him.

'For a moment I didn't say anything to Arnie, I was so surprised. I was thinking. You know Raymona, a goodbye isn't exactly like the end of story where you have to stuff everything in and make it the way you want it to be. Maybe a goodbye is just letting someone know you were with them for a while and you're glad of that. It doesn't have to make sense. It doesn't have to make everything all right either.

'Well, I invited Arnie over to come and visit next Friday night. It would be nice to see him again. How are you Raymona? How's that parrot doing?"

Goose bumps were popping up all over Raymona's naked body; it was either excitement or cold. To nurture that fragile bud of a story, Raymona said, "He died of asthma, you know, all that damp." But nothing worked. Matthew simply mentioned that he was going to the hardware store to pick up some woodwork polish. His voice disappeared.

Raymona stared out into her empty apartment, shocked. So close this time, so close. Still, there was a glimmer of hope; after all Arnie was coming to see Matthew on Friday night. She marked it on her calendar. All Friday she could feel the excitement mount. That evening she turned the volume of her TV and radio down; she didn't want to miss the call. Finally, finally Sunday evening the phone rang. She had already played the Jonah game eight times since Friday. Here fingers were permanently wrinkled like prunes.

She lifted the receiver with her damp hand.

"Hi Ramona, how are you?"

She decided that she wouldn't dignify that foolish question with an answer. Just as she was about to place the cell phone next to the blender, she heard a familiar intonation, like a far off clarion call.

"You know Raymona, it was just amazing...."

She placed the phone next to her ear. "How amazing, Matthew, tell me everything."

"Well, Friday evening, I was just putting the last

finishing touches on my Bulgarian cabbage soup, you know, from that recipe book Alphonso gave me a few years back...."

Raymona nodded frantically, not even asking who in the hell Alphonso was.

"Well, I had just realized that I forgot to buy sour cream. Why do all those Eastern Europeans eat so much sour cream anyway? Well I looked through my refrigerator and found an old jar of mayonnaise. I thought to myself, I bet that'll work; it's white after all."

Raymona, even fifteen hundred miles away was beginning to feel queasy. God it was wonderful!

"You'd know it, just as I was dropping big globs of mayonnaise into the soup, I hear the bell ringing. I ran and looked down from the porch, and it was Arnie!" Matthew gasped with excitement and absolute surprise.

Raymona silently picked up a pencil and drew a single line through the name "Arnie" written on her calendar.

"Well, I go downstairs to let him in. It was cold, and there he was standing in front of the door. He had a plaid green hunting cap on, and a green wool scarf wrapped all around his neck, one end of it was sticking out from back like he was some sort of horse with a green tail. Air was snorting out of his nose and mouth.

'I invited him in, and he smelled kind of smoky. His eyes looked right at me, not like they were going to slide away in a joke. Of course I wanted to be sympathetic and all, so I asked him how he was doing with loosing Dan. And you know Raymona, he just stood they're like he was paralyzed and couldn't say anything. He kept standing there for the longest time, and then I kind of guided him down to sit on the sofa. I gave him a little pat on the shoulder and was starting to feel pretty embarrassed because he seemed to kind of want something from me, but I didn't know what it was; so I decide to fix some tea, it being a cold night and all.

'Even when I'm banging around in the kitchen, he still didsn't say much except that he would like to have tea. I stayed in that kitchen a little longer than I had to, just trying to figure out what to do next. But when I come back, there he was just like I left him, all quiet and kind of waiting. So I sat next to him. I don't know why I sat so close to him...I just did. He even bounced up and down a little when I settled in place because I sat so close.

'So, I know this is crazy Raymona, but I put my hand on his shoulder and just leave it there. Then he took a deep breath and kind of shook a little. Then his whole body got so relaxed that he started leaning against me. You know Raymona, it's only after he relaxed that he started talking, real slowly, and it wasn't the words so much that mattered; it was something different, more like a melody; and we both just sat there for the longest while listening. I didn't realize how easy it was to just listen; I didn't have to do anything except be next to him.

'Then that kind of passed, and I asked him if he wanted to eat. He said yes, and so we got up and sat down in the kitchen. He said that he liked the soup, but wasn't too sure about the mayonnaise. The funny thing was, we both started laughing about that. I didn't feel embarrassed because we were laughing together. For a while we laughed so hard that we couldn't stop.

Isn't that strange Raymona? Here someone dies and we're laughing, and it's all right. I wish Dan and even James Arndt could have laughed with us. Do you know that James Arndt is going to take care of Trixie, and she's a pretty smelly dog?

'And then when we were all done with that laughing and had settled down, he said that it was time for him to go; he had to get up early the next morning. That was just fine by me. Then we stood up, and hugged each other; I could really feel his body next to mine, and he had a sort of smoky, wood smell. For a moment, I got a little worried about Lance and all, you know Lance being Arnie's partner, but then I felt all right, because I knew that everything was simple, just one thing at a time, like when I was in the Boundary Waters.

'He called me Sunday morning to thank me. I said 'never mind, it wasn't anything important.' He said that it was. And then we laughed again. He invited me to go out with him and Lance and this guy named Eric to listen to a Balkan accordion band, Tuesday next. Eric is a veterinarian."

Raymona's face was beginning to melt into a tentative satisfaction. Safety was dawning, and then just when things were getting good, Matthew spoiled it.

"How are you Raymona?"

Raymona was ready to deflect the attack. She once again could feel the eyes of the beast upon her.

But Matthew didn't seem to get the point; silence held sway over that phone line.

"Earth to Matthew, earth to Matthew, are you still alive?"

"Sure I'm alive Raymona. Well, I don't know much about Eric, except he's a friend of Arnie's."

Raymona's grip began tightening on the phone as if she were trying to squeeze more out of it. "So you're going on a blind date, with a guy who's into animals. Sounds like a good start Matthew."

"Well Raymona, I suppose he likes animals, being a veterinarian, but I don't think it's a date. It just sounds like fun, Balkan music and all."

"Oh Matthew, isn't that wonderful...seeing someone new. Who knows what can happen. Isn't that amazing Matthew?"

"I suppose so, but how are you Raymona, how are you doing?"

"I've got another call coming in." Raymona began reaching for the Kleenex box.

"Well, it's getting late Raymona; I'll just say goodbye."

She heard a click, and that nasty hornet sound. She couldn't believe it; Matthew left her THERE, THERE! just when she was beginning to feel safe again. She marked Eric's name on the calendar.

Wednesday night, just when she thought that she couldn't stand the suspense anymore; Matthew called.

She grasped the reins of the conversation. "Do you think cat's have souls Matthew?"

"Gee I'm not sure Raymona. How are you?"

"Tell me, tell me how it was with Eric. Any plans for future trips with him, maybe into the sunset?"

"I don't think so. I really can't go away for a while, I need to catch up on my business here a little, the accordion concert was pretty nice, and Eric was fun."

Raymona had finally had enough. "Matthew what's wrong with you? Fun, what kind of word is fun. I expect to hear that something wonderful or horrible happened to you. What's the world coming to when even you start to have fun?"

That's when he started laughing on the other end of the line, not a kind of cackling laugh that point's at someone in disdain, but a larger laugh that starts by sneaking through the nose and suddenly pushes all the way out, taking over the whole face and body until nothing else matters.

She was just imagining would it would sound like on his end of the line if she actually placed the phone in the blender, little bits of plastic scattering around the room, each little piece echoing, "How are you Raymona?"

Then even worse, laughter snuck up on her, or perhaps that funny little hair up her ass was squirming.

And then he said, hardly able to stop bursting, "I sure enjoy being with you, Raymona. You're lots of fun."

She didn't crunch popcorn in his ear. Maybe it was that she didn't want to choke to death; laughing so hard. After all when she died, she didn't want it to be an accident. She could see the obituary already, "She laughed so hard she accidentally choked to death on popcorn that she refused to stop eating."

Maybe it wouldn't be an accident. Maybe nothing is an accident anyway.

And then he said goodbye leaving her wondering about the possibility of a comet striking the east coast. The problem with never being absolutely sure if something is going to happen, is that you're never absolutely sure that something is not going to happen. So much for The Uncertainty Principle.

CHAPTER 17

There she was, in a fine state of affairs, actually answering the phone after two rings. She sat abandoned in her apartment, systems, rules, games... all diversions were for naught, like Job tested beyond endurance by a careless God. The Lord has given and the Lord has taken away; blessed be the name of the Lord...swell! She was that desperate for a story from Matthew.

Godzilla, tragedy in Bosnia, Noah, BAYWATCH, nothing distracted her. She didn't even know what Eric looked like. Of all the stupid things...two days after Matthew's aborted attempt at a story, she answered her cell phone after one ring. After all, now she was truly living in uncertainty.

"Hello my bubala."

And who was it, but her uncle Mel, gorgeous Mel Weinstein. A few years back you could see him on New York cable, hair, what was left of it, all slicked forward introducing MEL'S AFTERNOON MOVIE MATINEE. As if introducing the movie wasn't bad enough, somewhere midway through that old movie, his face would flash on the screen. This was supposed to be an intermission, and anyone watching, had the privilege to spend that intermission with Mel. For ten minutes he'd tell everybody stranded in front of their television sets, how he used to schmooz around in Hollywood with Betty Davis or Kirk Douglas...good old Mel had never been west of the Hudson River.

"Raymona my darling, my lovely grand daughter Buffy is having her Bat Mitspha, all of us want you to come."

"Dear Uncle Mel, why should I be so happy that this kid is finally grown up and going out into a world that's ready to eat her up."

"But my darling, life is like that. You think it's a bowl of cherries?"

As if that was any sort of an answer...she was about to put the telephone in the microwave, when she had a brainstorm...why, Mel could tell her stories. So she said, "Enough already, I'll go." She knew that all she had to do was use the word "enough" and Mel would schmooze on forever.

"Did I ever tell you about the time I had breakfast with Ginger Rogers? I used to call her Ginny; only her best friends called her Ginny. She says, "Mel, I really need to talk with you. You gotta get a load of this." Raymona knew then and there that she needed, yes needed, to cultivate her relationship with Mel.

Raymona had a whole week to prepare for her dangerous outing and she needed a whole week too;

after all this would be her first social appearance in years. She knew this immanent and disasterous exodus was all Matthew's fault; he was the last sure thing that she knew, and now he had betrayed her. Now she actually had to go out of her apartment for a prolonged period of time in the fragile hope that she could keep Uncle Mel interested in her enough to keep those stories rolling. She was truly humbled. As for Matthew, he was yesterday's chopped liver.

She decided against wearing her old dashiki...that went out of style with the Black Panthers. Then she thought about that floor length formal her mother made her wear at college graduation, but when Raymona glanced at her self in the bathroom mirror, she looked like some demented drag queen out to earn spare change. She switched to a plaid shirt, conservative slacks, and birkenstocks, and suddenly she was this black dyke who was a vegetarian and very concerned about the situation in Guatemala. Each time she peeked into the mirror with a new costume on, she was reincarnated into a different life story. Everything she wore earned her a place in a parade where she'd be pulled through mobs of screaming people. Once you're in that parade, you're done for. You end up in a concentration camp or a slave ship or playing bingo all night at St. Mary's parish hall.

She sat down, exhausted by her transformations, and turned on her rap channel so loud that the booming base scrambled her brains. It was 2Pac, 2Pac doing electroshock treatment. Now there was a smart operator, his name hovered midway between a number and a word, like a missing link between self and abstraction. He wouldn't be caught like those Yorubas, and Ibos, and Mandingos captured and chained in bellies of ships, dying in their own piss. His words hovered between obscenity and idealism like the crushed glass his ancestors slipped into the master's gravy.

Or maybe he was just a smart ass. His rap pounded through the radio in waves of defiance that made white suburban kids want to wear baggy pants and hope someday to be that angry too. 2Pac was her man.

That's it, she'd step onto the streets of New York as a rapping phenomenon: stocking cap, sunglasses, big baggy shirt, and pants slipping down her butt...she'll go hip hop. She'll fade in and be part of the street action, real cool, so cool that she'd just be an attitude..."whatcha looking at mothafucka?"

She stood in the bathroom, kind of rocking on her heels, hands buried deep in her imaginary pockets. With a scowl on her face she looked straight at that terrifying bathroom mirror, and began her very own rap incantation.

"Whatcha lookin' at mothafucka, mothafucka?
Whatcha lookin' at mothafucka, mothafucka?
Don't make no moves, don't try no shit,
Don't stick your hand on either a my tits,
Ya man, ya man
I'm a real cool chic
With a real cool trick
You watch your step, prick
I ain't bad, I ain't rude,

I got attitude.
Whatcha lookin' at mothafucka, mothafucka?
Whatcha lookin' at mothafucka, mothafucka?"

CHAPTER 18

The day of her destiny dawned. She took one last, long steamy bath, and carefully pulled on clean panties; they had to be clean because her jeans would be at half mast. She even strapped on a bra for protection. Finally loins girded, she slipped a stocking cap over her head, pulling it down to her sunglasses.

Time hung still and solemn as she ate what would probably be her last breakfast. She rang Matthew's number; a very tentative "hello?" filtered through Raymona's receiver, as if Matthew weren't sure that that's the right word to use when you pick up a phone. She hung up immediately.

She wrote one last testament to the world:

"To Whom, if Anybody, This May Concern,

I, Raymona Washington Goldberg, being of relatively sound body and mind, here bequeath my electrical appliances and phone to Matthew Pierson. I have fond memories of his voice whispering inane stories over the phone. I also want the world to know that my tragic death would not have occurred if he had not played so hard to get."

She wistfully took one last look at her tiny one room world, and then as she unbolted the locks on the door, her whole life flashed before her eyes. Trembling hand opening the door, she peeked her head out into the hallway...all clear. She stepped out, and released the door; it shut of its own accord, pushing her out. She heard the click of the automatic lock, and she knew that she was sealed out of her past forever.

She could feel the flushing rhythm of her heart drumming faster and faster in her ears. Valiantly she started repeating her mantra:

"Whatcha lookin' at mothafucka, mothafucka?

Whatcha lookin' at mothafucka, mothafucka?"

A stocking capped rap phenomenon, midway between self and attitude approached that final apartment door out into a dangerous world. She stopped in her tracks before that last portal, slid her pants and inch further down her butt, and began rolling her hips in an approximation of a street strut. Just as "Whatcha lookin' at mothafucka, mothafucka" was whispering through her lips, Martha who lived in the apartment across the hall walked through that front door holding a paper cup full of coffee which she had just bought from the Greek coffee shop next door.

This was a moment of truth for Raymona; would she be recognized for the street smart gangsta that she really was?

Martha, who was an insurance copywriter, switched

the coffee from her right hand to her left. She needed her right hand free to scratch her head. "Raymona, you wouldn't believe what they charge for a cup of coffee now."

Raymona could hear the sound of irritated footsteps and slurpy sipping disappear down the hall.

Shaken, but undeterred by her exposure, Raymona lowered her pants yet further and stepped out of the door towards her doom. Muttering almost audibly now, she walked with her wobbling gait to the subway.

On the streets of old New York, life was going on as usual, as if this weren't the Final Day. Raymona noticed the big fat roasted turkey in the deli window, and how Kay's Flowers and Gift Shop was filled with orchids. For a moment she was glad that her last day would be before the holidays. The world out here was full of smells: pizza, and strong perfume from the woman who just passed by, garbage from the big old metal container heating up in the brief winter sun, and even urine just around the corner where some one probably spent the night. And sounds, so many sounds, kids laughing and car horns squawking and the rumble that comes from the city any time of day.

This is it; this is what she feared all along. Sensations exploded in her body, reaming her out and demolishing her control; feet and lips kept moving with a life of their own. For an instant, gone was 2Pac, gone even was Raymona. Nature which abhors a vacuum had to fill those lips with something. Was it some racial memory, or a flashback to the freedom bus? As her eyes bounced around her head, her lips formed the words of a different song:

"Sometimes I feel like a motherless child,
Sometimes a feel like a motherless child,
Sometimes I feel like a motherless child,
A long way from home."

Those words muttered through her lips as her ears pounded, and her breath squeezed out in shallow little gasps. She had to keep her focus, she had to keep her focus or she'd shatter into a million screaming pieces. She tried to force herself back to rap. "Sometimes I feel like a motha fucka, motha fucka,

Whatcha lookin' at motherless child a long way from home

Don't make no moves, don't try no shit,
Hava, Nagila Hava.
Hail Mary full of grace,
You watch your step, I'll smack you in the face!"
We shall overcome, we shall overcome
You ass hole lickin' bum."

Her lips kept conjuring up pieces of those hated stories from her past. Songs and complaints that she had stuffed so far down that even she couldn't remember them, were bubbling up. The voices of her past were escaping through her mouth.

Now she was at the entrance of the subway, her Underground Railroad. Raymona stepped down those stairs that descended into a darkness that roared and squealed and blew hot air from hell into her face. Harriet Tubman replaced 2Pac on Raymona's lips:

"Go down, Moses
Way down in Egypt land
Tell ole Pharaoh
To let my people go, mothafucka, mothafucka."

Her feet tripped up on one of those stairs; she grabbed the handrail and took the dark glasses off... she reached the shadowy bottom. Still hoping to salvage some cool, she put a limping strut back into her stride and walked over to a glassed in booth in which a man who never looked up, sat counting change. Tentatively she pushed her money through a smooth depression under the glass. The equal opportunity gate keeper to hell flicked her a token without loosing his count. She walked into the metal arms of a gate and deposited her token. It pulled her through to the Other Side.

Her lips were silent now; she was in the heart of terror. The world of apartments and television and food and daylight and phones had disappeared. Shadowy people like herself waited in that dark nowhere tunnel staring vacantly at the empty tracks as if their desperation were a way out. Then a far off rumble started; rotten air from inside the dark cavern from which that ominous sound erupted started rushing through the tunnel like an angel of doom. The rumble turned into a scream that shattered even despair into smithereens; the beast with the yellow eye charged into the tunnel and stopped at Raymona's feet. Dull metal doors slid open...doom.

What was left of Raymona was now hovering above her body, trying to stop it from stepping into that metal horror, but that dumb form of hers walked through that opening and dragged her with it. The doors closed; she sat on one of those glossy benches that lined both sides of the car; she closed her eyes. The monster roared, lurch forward and set off with her in its belly.

She prepared to die. After a few expectant moments, eyes squeezed shut, she realized that that roaring sound reminded her of her blender, when she put ice cubes in it. That fragile self of hers again woke in her body... she opened her eyes.

Even the dull light of the subway station had disappeared from behind the window that she faced. A black wall on the other side streamed by that would skin her nose and then smash her head if she thought about it. Light had gone from the world outside, and the glass of the window was now a mirror.

Raymona studied that form of herself sitting opposite in that mirror, stocking cap pulled over a black face with a mouth open like a dead fish. That was herself, that was herself...it had come to this. The subway pulled into another station. There was light on the other side of the window now, and that spooky self of hers disappeared. The metal doors slid open.

A black man walked through those doors, with a kind of roll in his stride and eyes almost as spooky as Raymona's. He was wearing blue pants that once upon a time must have been part of somebody's leisure suite. He had this skimpy little jacket on that he probably got from a thrift shop or from somebody who didn't like him very much. His eyes had a funny kind of pleading look, like he couldn't stop apologizing for just being alive; a man the world is suspicious of. But still he had that walk down, real natural.

The subway set off again down the dark tunnel. Once more she stared at that dead fish of herself sitting opposite her.

"Hey sister what you looking at, you look scared to death."

She shot a quick scowl at him, and then turned back to the fish. She watched the fish's mouth start moving. "Whatcha lookin at mothafucka, mothafucka, whatcha lookin at mothafucka, mothafucka."

"Just aksed you a question I ain't gonna hurt you."

His pleading tone calmed her enough to allow her to glance over at him. He was a brother all right, one of those men who look like they're having a hard time that doesn't quit. She mumbled, "I was just looking at myself."

That pleading voice of his was replaced by a kind of no nonsense, don't-talk-shit-to-me-now kind of tone. "What you talkin' about? Your eyes are inside your head."

Now, Raymona didn't like questions. In fact, if she had been in her own tiny realm, at this point she would have used one of her electrical appliances to chastise or at least evade this importunate suitor; but here she was, no sunglasses and exiled from all she knew. All she could do in explanation was to point to that dead fish sitting opposite her who had captured her attention.

For a minute he looked back and forth from her to her. "You need some education sister. The one that breathes is you. Don't you feel that bench under your backside?"

Sure enough those two butt bones of hers were rocking against that hard seat, and her breath was lifting her chest in sharp little gasps. She could breathe, in fact something inside took a big gulp of air that turned into a yawn. Then because of that real skimpy jacket of his, she decided to cut him a break.

"Hey brotha what you doin' out here?"

For a moment it was his turn to get real embarrassed like he was caught in the midst of doing something wrong and he better have a pretty good excuse on hand. Then without shifting into attitude, he smoothed out, like he was remembering something, maybe even feeling his own butt bones rocking on the seat. He said, "Bin seeing my girlfriend, now I'm going to work. I got me this big building I have to watch over at night." He nodded and kind of sucked in his lips a little. "It's a big old building; I started there a ways back." He looked up at Raymona as if he were taking her measure or at least making sure she didn't think he was in the wrong place.

Raymona paused and then nodded her head as if she were really taking this all in. "At least you're gettin' out on a regular basis. I only get out when I have to. All kind of craziness goes on out here."

"You can say that again sister!" He started laughing through a big old gap in his teeth. "A ways back I got me all caught up in that. Now I got me a good job and a girlfriend that's real steady. Sometimes I start thinking that craziness has my name on it and I just might as well get all messed up again, but then I say to myself 'Lawrence you stay out of there. Enough brothas gone that way. You'll spend all your time just being what the man says you are.'" He looked at Raymona and shook his head like he knew that she was indeed a sister and would know what he was talking about.

Those metal doors opened again and let in people from Mid Town, fancy looking busy people, dressed up for parades. The subway roared on. Lawrence and Raymona nodded to each other once and a while between all those prosperous people staring silently at their reflections. Even those dark gaps in his teeth didn't seem so bad.

Further up on the West side, Lawrence stood up; those doors opened again. He looked at Raymona just before he stepped outside. He didn't even seem to care if the other's heard him. "Sometimes I just want to hang out on the street again sister, hang out where they know my name; you don't know how hard I want to sometimes."

They looked at each other deep down for a moment, then he stepped out to go to that building of his. She watched him stroll all elegant into that station, like he was showing her how to do it. The doors clanged shut, she sped into the dark tunnel, hardly noticing that hip hop chic in the window.

CHAPTER 19

The train now rushed upwards, and there was sky out the windows, a New York blue, thick and hazy. The train wove its way through grimy brick apartment buildings with metal gates behind the windows. Raymona could see dark kids sitting down after school, televisions flashing in their faces. One small boy was looking straight out his caged window on the second floor and waved. Without thinking, she waved back. For the briefest moment she felt some kind of instantaneous connection.

The train kept moving until it was no longer walled in by dirty brick, and clanged straight out over the river like some clumsy airplane, straight out into the New York blue. The sun was slipping down towards Jersey; it shone thru the train windows and lit up Raymona's face. The Hudson was all broad, flowing under her, like memories released and free to rush down into the ocean, an ocean whose water held all the experiences flowing into it.

Clanging, the train passed over the river and into

a brick canyon again, a place where stories had been fighting each other for years hardly bothering to take hostages, the Bronx. Survivors scurried around getting ready to duck into some building that may not be there anymore: a city turning into the surface of the moon. But when Raymona looked more closely in the last light of day, she saw boys playing basketball, and women talking on front stoops. Bodega's and hair salons and even Chinese restaurants were all still open for the business and pleasure of life. She felt it all.

Suddenly she remembered all those people waiting for her up ahead, the Weinsteins and Goldbergs and Greenbergs and Spielmans, all waiting to welcome her. Raymona had always hated being welcomed. She was sure all those reaching arms would only pull her down to destruction. Good old Buffy was being sent out into a world that would as soon gas you as let you be. The train was approaching Riverdale now...more trees, and people on the sidewalks were almost strolling.

Gently Raymona rocked back and forth from butt bone to butt bone, the train gently clanking. With each alternating, soft pressure on her back side, her eyes blinked. . .all clear. Her face, her whole body opened out, faster than the speed of light, taking in sensations like a lullaby, hushabye don't you cry. All the prayers and curses that had lain coiled up inside her released with each blink; finally leaving her sitting there, a woman in the evening, a woman with evening and sunlight and darkness rippling through.

She sat with the other passengers, not just those

stockbrokers and copywriters and secretaries sitting on the benches or standing while they held on to thick plastic straps. Her unwinding incantations had released a whole crowd of spirits whose miseries and joys and battles had filled the dreams and nightmares of her childhood.

That gray morning in her long ago childhood, she had said, "enough!" After that, anytime those voices started to seep out, she would plug her mouth and mind; terrified at the destruction her stories could unleash. It wasn't the beast outside that she was afraid of now… what was it…what was it…what was it? Yes, that's it? It was her fault…if only she silenced herself, hid herself, maybe everything would be all right. It wasn't herself she was protecting but the world. She had hid so completely that even she couldn't find herself. If she no longer inhabited herself the world would be, would be safe. That's what the brother on the train was trying to show her. She was still here on her butt bones! Life ran through her now.

And now they rode with her…Sojourner Truth, a white slaver, Albert Einstein, a Nazi guard, Francis of Assisi, Frederick Douglas, Anne Frank, Joseph McCarthy, Malcolm X...some trying to forget, some trying to remember what had happened; each a pebble that had been dropped in the pool of Raymona's mind, each pebble setting off an ever broadening ring. All those ripples crossing each other setting up interference patterns that seemed like chaos.

A broadening tumult rings of kindness and cruelty,

suffering and joy, horror and ecstasy all crisscrossed each other, creating a geography as meaningless as the surface of the moon...the beast, finally the beast, a calamity of meaninglessness that devours everyone after that brief season, that brief story in which victory seemed possible. The price some paid for that brief victory, the price other people suffered.

She got off at the Riverdale and began walking. People weren't scurrying around as much up here. Bars were hardly visible in the glass windows of stores behind which were shiny nice things, trophies for winning. Even the Laundromat was all lit up like there was a party taking place under glass. Children drank sodas, and mothers in an underwater ballet folded clothes. There in the corner, a woman in a lime green dress leaned against the window reading, creating a lime green decal on the glass. For a moment Raymona wanted to touch that lime green and feel whatever was going on in there.

Then she saw that familiar hip hop chic in the darkened window of a dry cleaning store, matching Raymona's pace. Raymona made a half hearted attempt to stuff her mouth with rap, but the last bits of jumble slipped out: Virgin Mary's and mothafuckas and Kaddish and spirituals: prayers and curses so mixed up that they had turned Raymona's mind into the surface of the moon.

Just as her eyes were beginning to glass over, she remembered her butt bones. That's when she heard her steps against the sidewalk in beat, not hip hop, but still a beat that penetrated now and then and will be.

Go down, Moses,
Way down in Egypt Land
Tell ole Pharaoh
To let my people go.

While that beat drummed through her, she heard her breath in soft syncopation whispering...

Yisgadal, V'yeskadash
Sh'mei Rabbaw.

Those two beats danced in and out of each other, and then a third beat joined them. Her heart flushed blood through her body...

Blessed are
The poor in spirit
For theirs
Is the kingdom of heaven.

All three beats now joined. Then another beat began...

I was a hidden treasure.
I would fain be known.
So I created Man."
There is no God
But Allah.

All four beats joined in complex syncopation, sometimes canceling each other out, sometimes creating a beat so big it took Raymona's breath away. The surface of the moon, meaningless except for the laser of her awareness creating the holographic experience of self, all there still there, and only she could cast that spell.

And while a radio played Reggae through an open window, and a police car screamed as it was speeding to the scene of a murder, and a child hummed some repeating melody while she sat on the front step, and two people exchanged kisses, and a sparrow tittered... each passed through Raymona joining the other rhythms, and as each passed through her, or really as she shone through her a world, she created a self that only she could and share.

The beast, the beast of meaningless chaos, was just an interference pattern of all the hopes and horrors, tragedies and failures, kindness and cruelties. But when her life streamed through that frozen moment, music and images flowed in an individual rhythm that moved out in broadening rings to join the beat of the universe. Each beat burst open the frozen world of the masters and guards.

Raymona listened carefully; she thought she could still hear distant sighs and screams and laughter, all of it still there drumming, expanding, beyond any blessing and song, praise and consolation that are uttered in the world.

CHAPTER 20

It was late November in Minnesota. The time of the year there, when no one with any sense believes that spring will ever come again. Lakes were already frozen shut. Young children could hardly believe that the summer world had come to this.

It was after nine now. Matthew was still up. The phone rang. He finished the sentence he was reading, placed the book on the brown cushion next to him and reached for the phone. "Hello?"

"Matthew this is Raymona."

"Raymona?"

"Ramona."

"RAYMONA?"

"Are you an echo or something?"

"Raymona, I just didn't think you'd call…ever. That's amazing!"

"Did anyone ever tell you that you're easily amazed?"

"Well people have said I'm spacy, but I don't know if that's the same thing. How are you Raymona?"

"Do I have something to tell you! Well, I just

finished riding on the subway with Paul Robeson, Golda Meir, Pope John XXIII, Adolf Eichman, Martin Luther King and Mohammed."

"Wow, that's amazing Raymona!"

"I thought you'd say that. Aren't you going to ask me why all those people were on the subway, especially since they're dead?"

"Now that you mention it, why were all those people on the subway, being dead and all?"

"Well, I was going to Buffy Weinstein's Bat Mitspha."

"Oh, sure, you told me you were going, but..."

"Butt, that's what it's all about Matthew."

"It is?"

"It's this way Matthew, I'm sitting right now and I can feel pressure on my butt. And since I can feel that pressure, I have a pretty good shot at hearing myself breath. And hearing myself breathe, if I listen even more carefully I can hear my heart beat. Do you get the drift, Matthew?"

Long tentative pause..."I suppose so."

"Well, as soon as I hear all that, presto, I'm aware that I'm in this chair. I hear my refrigerator, and then I know I'm in this room. I hear traffic outside, and then I know I'm in New York. And then I look through the smog and I see a star, and I know I'm in the universe. Then I'm all of everything, because everything is passing through me like I'm a funnel. Horrible stuff can still happen, but I'm so big, in some funny way, it's all just part of me. Do you understand Matthew? When I start listening and feeling, and seeing, and smelling I spread out to everywhere. Even those infomercials where people say their lives have been totally transformed by eating a diet candy bar don't seem so bad. Do you get it Matthew?"

There's another long pause at the other end, finally, "I did see this one commercial where this guy was selling something that looked like a can of spray paint. He sprayed the bald spots in the back of men's heads. And it was some sort of paint. After these guys got the backs of their heads painted, they said their lives were changed. Some of their wives cried for joy and the audience clapped and cheered. Is that what you mean Raymona?"

"That's part of it Matthew. But you didn't get anything about the spreading out?"

"Um, no I don't think so, Raymona. I'm not as deep as you. You know you ought to see the moon here Raymona. It's big and yellow, and the sky is so clear. It makes me just want to sail away with it."

There was a full minute of silence in the universe, and it wasn't filled with games or stories. Finally Raymona spoke, "I got you, Matthew. You go ahead and sail away. When you come back, tell me about it, or even better, I'll meet you there.

THE END

www.ingramcontent.com/pod-product-compliance
Ingram Content Group UK Ltd.
Pitfield, Milton Keynes, MK11 3LW, UK
UKHW040007200726
13854UKWH00001B/86

9 798887 032610